Madly,

Deeply

ERICA CROUCH

MADLY, DEEPLY
Copyright © 2014, Erica Crouch

First Edition.
ISBN: 1927940052
ISBN-13: 9781927940051

Patchwork-Press.com

To my befores, and all of my afters.

Part 1

It was many and many a year ago,
In a kingdom by the sea,
That a maiden there lived whom you may know
By the name of Annabel Lee;
And this maiden she lived with no other thought
Than to love and be loved by me.

— Stanza I, *Annabel Lee* by Edgar Allan Poe

CHAPTER 1

A Proposal

ANNALEIGH WELLS WAS A PHANTOM on the shore watching the fog. Her shadowed silhouette waxed and waned from her waist to her full dress, and her pale hair, which had been painstakingly piled on her head that morning, was coming undone in ringlets that framed her small face in a halo of gold.

Dense, low-hanging clouds drifted across the lake, waltzing in time with the wind. They eddied and stretched inches above the unbroken glass of water. The fingers of fog ran so achingly close to the surface that Annaleigh was sure they'd connect. She willed them to meet, to touch another just once. But always, the mist and the water—two lovers divided by the thinnest of veils—pulled back at the last second, inseparably alone.

She took a step forward, toeing the lapping edge of the water with satin boots. From across the lake, she could just barely make out the indistinct shape of the wooden dock, its planks warped with dampness.

A dark, cawing raven disappeared into the haze, and the clouds dove down on a breeze. Annaleigh sucked in her breath, holding the air in her lungs until the mist caressed the water. But before the elements brushed into one, an arm wrapped around her middle, spinning her quickly from the shore and whisking away her breath.

The world was a blur of gray, orange, and blue. Fog, leaves, sky. Cinching her eyes closed, she waited for the ground beneath her feet to steady itself again. Only when her back found the rough solidity of a tree trunk did she open her eyes again, just to be met with more gray.

"Dammit, William James Calloway!"

"You shouldn't stand so close to the water," he whispered, leaning into the crook of her warm neck. He spoke the words to the rhythm of her pulse, one by one. "You could fall in and drown. What would I do with myself then?"

His eyes were the same shade as the autumn fog, dark and filled with mischief and secrets. Often, he'd used them to render Annaleigh incoherent, realizing the effect a held gaze could have on her continence.

Everything about William was ink and scarlet, dark hair and wind-bitten aristocratic cheeks. He possessed a posture that had been carved from arrogance, but between the sharp angles of his shoulders were a deep thoughtfulness and a tender heart that beat too hard and too fast for those he loved. He was dangerous and reckless when he fell in love.

How long had he been searching for her?

Annaleigh pushed him back, halfheartedly swatting at his shoulder. "Find someone else to scare, I'd imagine."

"I scared you, did I?" A slow grin overtook his face like a languid winter sunrise, bright and cool.

"Startled," she corrected. "I'm not afraid of anything."

"Of course not." He grazed his gloved hand across her shoulder, fingering the collar of her coat. His thumb traced her collarbone. "You smell like snow, Annaleigh."

"*You* smell of wine, cinnamon, and smoke. Did you have dessert without me?"

"Wouldn't dream of it."

The space between them closed and he kissed her into the curve of the tree, pressing her to nature. The dying leaves of the tree reached toward them, greedy to hide their new companions from the world.

Annaleigh walked her hands up the front of his coat, stopping when she hit something solid beneath the sturdy material. She parted from his lips to breathe a question.

"What's in your pocket?" she asked.

He briskly patted the chest of his coat, then a pocket at his waist, and shrugged. "Nothing."

She placed a bare finger on his lips before he could kiss her again. "What are you hiding from me?" She arched her eyebrow in a delicate curve.

"It's simply a Christmas present."

"Impossible. You wait until Christmas Day to find gifts."

Space—cold and empty—grew between them as he pulled away from her and turned to face the lake. "You'll learn I'm full of surprises."

Annaleigh straightened from the tree, and the leaves shuddered in the wind above them. She was not one to simply see a fiction and let it pass as truth, and William was easy to read. He had no way to mask his fibs around her. The lie lived in his dimpled smile, which was just a little too wide. It sparked to life behind his traitorous eyes.

"What's in your pocket, William?" she pressed forward.

He took a step back, his grin going lopsided in amusement. For every step she took toward him, he paced back, a dance of curiosity and secrets.

"William!"

She sped up her pace until they were spinning around one another, the world beyond their game nothing but smudged winter. He reached out, clasped her hand, and pulled her waist close to his, formalizing their movements into something that belonged in a ballroom.

For a moment, Annaleigh pretended to forget the game, resting her hand on his shoulder and mimicking proper form. But on the next spin, she let her hand slide down his lapel and slip inside his pocket. Before he realized what was happening, she tripped away from him, whisking back into the seclusion behind the curtain of leaves.

It was a box he had hidden from her—a blue velvet box that was nearly as large as her palm. She measured the weight of it, trying to guess what he had hidden inside.

A trick, she suspected. Some kind of prank to get another laugh out of her, or perhaps it was meant for his sister, Mary. Last year, he had rigged a present to spring out of its package when opened, scaring Mary so badly she had fallen out of her chair and spilled all of her wine down the front of her dress. She would have had William's head if his true gift to her hadn't been a new gown.

She shook the box carefully before cracking open its lid, worried about whatever might pop out. When she was confident there was nothing menacing inside, she opened it fully.

"Annaleigh, wait—" William ran up to her just as she was taking in the contents of his secret gift, his feet stopping when he saw her. The playful grin he was wearing froze before slipping into a look of nervousness.

In her hands, she held a locket, beautiful and intricate. Never in her life had she seen something as perfectly crafted. The metal was thin but sturdy, twisted into a pattern that resembled the sea. There was a small flower in the middle with petals that seemed to reach out like the rays of the sun, and she could swear there was the shape of a bird hidden within the complicated metalwork. She traced it with her finger and looked up at William's shocked face.

"What is this?"

"You weren't supposed to see that. Not yet," William said.

She looked back down at the locket, touching the thin chain that rested on its plush pillow inside the box.

"It was my mother's. My father bought it for her when they were traveling in India, just after they married." He took a few steps forward, patting another one of his pockets with anxious fingers.

Annaleigh watched his movements, trying to pin the source of his nerves. Was it from talking about his mother, who had passed nearly five years ago? It was a topic he usually avoided. Or were his nerves sprouting from somewhere else? She wasn't sure.

"Mary held on to it after she died," he said, "but she could never wear it. When she was younger, she was convinced it was haunted. My mother would tell her bedtime stories about the magic it possessed. She told her tales of souls living inside it, of life after life."

Annaleigh traced the cool, metal waves of the locket's face.

"Mother was always telling Mary ghost stories, stirring up trouble with her imagination," William continued. "Father tried to explain that they were just that—stories. It was just the eternal nature of love, that the powers it held were a legend told by the old man who had sold it to him. He didn't think it meant much, but my mother—and Mary—did." He shrugged shyly, ran a nervous hand through his hair. "I thought you would like it. You were not meant to open it until after…"

Annaleigh raised her eyes to his. The danger that normally lived within him had disappeared; instead, tenderness had taken up residence. The way he looked at her gave flight to the butterflies in her stomach, fluttering wings tickling her from the inside out until she matched the nervousness that lived inside William in that moment.

"Why are you so infuriatingly curious?" He reached out and swept her fallen hair behind her ear, his hand lingering on her jaw.

"I find answers more rewarding than questions," she said, her voice quiet and shaking.

He lifted the locket and snapped its box closed, returning it to his front pocket. With tentative fingers, he unclasped the chain and moved to place it around her neck. The pendant was heavy around her neck, and it hung low, resting in the dip of her chest.

"It's beautiful, William." Annaleigh touched the locket with her hand, letting the coldness of the metal bite into her skin. The cold was a strange, pleasurable pain, and it calmed her.

"This," he said cautiously, reaching into his pocket to present a second, smaller velvet box to her, "was supposed to be hidden inside."

Bending down to one knee, he opened the box. For the second time that day, William stole away Annaleigh's breath.

Her cold hands found her mouth as her heart fought to escape her ribcage. It was only the bones of her corset that kept her from falling apart.

In the smaller box rested a ring. The band was simple—a bronze that almost appeared rosy in this lighting—but the setting was as ornate as the locket. It held six small diamonds, spaced like petals. A pale-blue gem rested at the center of the flower, bright and hopeful. It was the same color as her eyes, she distantly realized.

This was not an heirloom that had been passed down through the Calloway family tree; this had been specially made for her, designed by William. She could see the influences from the necklace, could feel the same spirit of love and life.

"William." Her gasp was as thin as the fog that still spun over the lake.

"Annaleigh Elizabeth Wells, you have filled my yesterdays with so much hope and love that every today feels like magic. I want to spend tomorrow with you. I want to spend every tomorrow for the rest of my life, and whatever life comes after this, loving you. I want the angels to watch us with envy, to dream that they might one day understand another as much as you do me and I you."

His eyes studied every feature on her face, committing them to memory. He spent an eternity counting the freckles that dusted the tops of her cheeks like newly fallen snow. Infinite moments were given to her eyes, her nose, her cheeks, her lips before he could speak again.

"Ours is a love that is stronger than any other I know. I don't need to be older or wiser about the world to realize that I have found my everything in you. I see you in the stars that survive the day, in the brazen tide of the sea at night. Before you, everything was dull and colorless. It's you who has made the earth beautiful. You saved my life."

Annaleigh's hand moved from her mouth down to the locket again. She felt the careful wings of the bird beneath her fingers, the curl of the waves, and she could swear she felt a warmth coming from within. It was the warmth of an embrace, of a peaceful night spent next to a fire. It was the warmth of William's love that lived within this necklace, the promise of forever.

"Nothing—not man, nor angels or demons—could dissever us. I will never leave your side, for our souls have entwined so completely that we are one. If you will have me as a husband, I would give my life to make you my wife." With one last deep breath, he gathered his courage, found his feet, and stood to look into her shining eyes. "Annaleigh, will you do me honor of marrying me?"

CHAPTER 2

A Reply

THERE WAS NO HESITATION IN her mind or her heart.

"For today, tomorrow, and the rest that follow, William. I am and always will be yours," she said, her voice breaking over her words. "In this life and the next."

She threw herself at him, knocking him off balance. Her arms wrapped around his neck and she clung to him like the last stubborn leaves in fall gripped the trees, refusing to let go no matter how furious the wind blew.

It seemed to take William several heartbeats before he realized her answer. He stood still, his breath caught in his chest, unsure whether she was a figment of his imagination or something else entirely. After a moment, though, he tightened his arms around her.

She wasn't a phantom of his imagination; she was real, she was here, and she'd said yes. His heart beat against her feverishly fast and strong.

There was an extreme happiness that warmed the space between them and filled Annaleigh's small frame with so much emotion she thought she would overflow. If it weren't for his grip on her, she would have spilled to the ground and sunk down to water the roots of the ancient tree that stood sentry behind her.

When William pulled back, he was wearing a grin so wide she was sure his face would split in two. There was still a hint of disbelief in his eyes, but the mischief was back. "I knew you would say yes."

She pushed his shoulders back. "Careful, or I'll take it back. I don't have a ring on my finger yet," she said, flourishing her bare fingers at him.

"I will have to rectify that immediately." He snatched her hand and pressed a kiss to her knuckles. With great care, he took the ring from its box and slid it onto her finger.

It fit perfectly and felt as if it had always belonged on her. It gave William a swell of pride to see her wearing the ring, tying them together in a more obvious way. He had always felt a sense of belonging with Annaleigh, and he'd hoped she felt the same for him, but their connection was invisible to the world beyond them. This was his love, his complete belonging, taking physical form. This was his promise of forever.

"Mary will be furious," he said, lacing his fingers with hers.

Together, they left the fog of the lake to walk up the soft, green hill back to the house. The gloom receded behind them as they climbed above the low clouds that hung over the water. It was like ascending from Earth into Heaven. The sky was heavy with the promise of snow, the early moon masked by a quilt of clouds.

"Our engagement was meant to happen on Christmas Eve," he continued. "Midnight. She had planned the whole thing, from when I would bend to one knee and what I was meant to say. Don't tell her I forgot the sonnet she made me memorize for the occasion—she'll never let me hear the end of it."

"A sonnet?" Annaleigh's mouth curved into a grin she'd tried to keep hidden. William had never been one for poetry unless, of course, Annaleigh was the one reciting it. Maybe if she prompted Mary later this evening, she could get him read it to her.

"I know. You would have seen right through that."

She laughed. "I would have immediately known something was amiss."

"But Mary insisted. She even wanted to be the one to wrap the necklace herself and then suggest that we each open one present early. I don't think she trusted me not to be utterly useless when it came to asking for your hand. If you had said no, she never would have forgiven me. She's always wanted a sister."

Annaleigh smiled to herself. She had already thought of Mary as a sister. The time they'd spent together—be it shopping in town or telling secrets late at night by candlelight—had made her wish that she had been closer with her own sisters growing up. But the age difference had separated her from her three older siblings, who had all married and moved away from home before her tenth birthday.

"How should I make it up to her, then?"

"Oh, I'm sure you'll think of something," William said, walking up stone steps in front of the house and pushing open the heavy doors.

CHAPTER 3

A History

THE CALLOWAY HOUSE, WHICH SHOULD be more rightly called an estate due to its grandeur in size and pasture, had been inherited from William's great-grandfather. It was three times as large as the one Annaleigh had grown up in closer to town, with much more stone and wood.

There were fireplaces large enough to walk into while standing up—which she only considered doing once after a particularly icy winter—and a large sweeping staircase that Mary had insisted having the Calloway family stand on, poised and proper, to have their portrait painted every year. Some portraits were of just her and William; one was just her. But last year, she had invited Annaleigh to join in the portrait, and William's smile had returned, the frame filling with joy once again.

"You're practically my sister, Anna," she'd shouted from the top of the staircase. She slid down the banister and landed clumsily in front of her before there was a chance to protest. "We're just waiting for Will and his stubborn mind to catch up. But you're already a Calloway, just not in name yet. You are family, and this is a *family* portrait. It wouldn't be complete without you."

A Calloway. It was a powerful name, and soon, it would belong to her, too. She wondered how she'd uphold such a heavy history.

William's family had helped found the town nearly a century ago, and their house was as stately as their name. His father, George, was an industrialist who had married the daughter of a rival businessman after amassing enough wealth to grow restless for more power. Their marriage combined two founding families' wealth to build a sizable estate—one of the most impressive in the country, Annaleigh would bet.

Before the rehearsals for their wedding, George and Sara Calloway hadn't even met, but according to stories told by Mary, they'd fallen immediately and incredibly in love. Sara was easily to fall in love with, and as soon as George met her, he was hopeless.

Their engagement was the talk of the town, but they couldn't have cared less—all they heard, all they saw, was one another. No one existed for him but her, from that moment on.

When Mary and William were growing up, they traveled with their parents all over Europe. They spent a majority of their education in France when they were still young enough to need a mother and a father to watch over them. They visited Asia, Africa, England—anywhere their hearts desired exploring.

By the time William turned thirteen, though, the children were sent back to America to complete their studies and apprenticeships. Being raised by nannies and cooks in a giant home while their parents explored the world beyond them was lonely for two children still so young. Perhaps that's what drew them together.

There was no parent to soothe a nightmare or tame a particularly dreadful fever. Mary only had William, and he only ever had her. Until William met Annaleigh one muggy summer evening down by the lake. He had caught her swimming, and she yelled at him for a good hour about his indecent stares. After that, they became fast friends, the first true friend William had had—the two Calloway children hadn't realized there were children their age so close to home.

They also had no idea of their wealth or worldliness. Money was nothing to them, and on multiple occasions, Annaleigh had to explain to Mary—who would slip into a string of fast, foreign syllables when frustrated—that she couldn't understand what she was saying because she couldn't speak French.

Even though neither Mary nor William would ever need to work due to their family's sizable fortune, George insisted both of his children have the intelligence and expertise to live, should everything suddenly disappear. But the money never dwindled—there was no threat of either children or parents becoming destitute and living on the street.

The only thing the Calloways had ever lost in their entire history, it would seem, was Sara. Before her death, they had not known loss; worry had been a distant ship waiting for them on the horizon, a threat that would never drop anchor. It wasn't supposed to come to shore so suddenly.

William never spoke about his mother if he could help it. Annaleigh had learned not to push him with questions about her. It was always Mary who mentioned Sara and kept her memory alive; she spoke of her mother like she was still in the room, sitting right next to her on the couch. Remembering what he'd lost was too painful for William. Every time Mary would start talking about her mother, he would subtly leave the room.

After Sara had died—consumption, the doctor had said—the light in George's eyes vanished. That day, William and Mary had lost not only a mother, but also their father. What had once been a strong, robust man withered away, carved thin by grief. His cheeks hollowed, his shoulders collapsed forward.

Without his wife, he could find no enthusiasm for life, no affection for his children. William had once mentioned in passing that he could count on one hand the number of times his father had hugged him as a boy. Ever since hearing that, Annaleigh had made sure to hug him more times than he'd ever be able to tally.

George, without Sara, was a man made of misery and regret. His memories only darkened the home where his children had been born, taken their first steps, and laughed. The vestige of Sara—her on the staircase, in their bedroom, singing in the parlor—was too much. Everything gave him nightmares. Her lingering presence ruined him.

The autumn of William's fifteenth birthday, George left for Europe. For sixteen months, he sent no word to his children, save for curt letters on birthdays and Christmas.

William said nothing to Annaleigh about his absence, but she could tell something was wrong. His jokes turned sour in his mouth; his laugh sounded hollow. He lied with smiles and shrugs any time she pushed him for the truth.

Eventually, he stopped coming by Annaleigh's. Even Mary wouldn't visit as often as she once had, and the few times she did, she was reserved. So unlike herself. Mary's own silence became too great for her to bear, and before long, she just stopped visiting altogether.

The two children—who had been forced to leave childhood behind much too early—retreated back into their giant house of maids and servants and solitude. The thick curtains were pulled over every tall window. All rooms were extinguished of any light. The house became a hulking shadow shrouded in grief and secrets, perched above the lake.

Outside, the garden and the grass died and the paint began to peel on the sunbaked front porch. The parties stopped; the celebrations died. No one came; no one went. There were no visitors except for the occasional delivery of milk and eggs by delivery boys who were nervous to walk the jagged, overgrown path to the eerie estate.

It didn't take long before rumors began in town that the Calloways' home was haunted. If Annaleigh hadn't known better, she would have believed it.

After one month without so much as a note from either Mary or William, Annaleigh marched up to their great house and knocked on the door as forcefully as she could. Samuel, who had worked for the Calloways since William was born, answered the door and told her that they weren't seeing anyone.

"Well, I'm not leaving, so you can tell them I'll just wait here until they *are* seeing people again."

"I'm afraid, Ms. Wells—"

She yelled this time, hoping her voice would echo loudly up the wooden stairs to their bedrooms. "It is my birthday, William! Aren't you at least going to say hello?"

A click and a shuffle later, William was standing at the top of the staircase, looking down at her. His hair was disheveled, his shirt untucked and wrinkled. There were dark circles under his eyes that made him look years older than he was.

"Happy birthday," he said, his voice as spare as his appearance. How much weight had he lost? Were they making sure he was eating?

Annaleigh crossed her arms and ignored the open door Samuel gestured her toward. "No. It's not."

"Excuse me?" William asked, surprised.

"You're not going to come down here and wish me a happy birthday? I have to look all the way up there at you, yell from here?"

Annaleigh wanted to stomp her foot, but she wouldn't give him the satisfaction of seeing her throw a tantrum like some child. She knew the Calloways kept to themselves—they'd much rather pretend everything was fine than admit they needed help, that something was wrong and they couldn't handle it on their own. They didn't know how to reach out for help, because they never had anyone to reach for before. It had only always been the two of them. William and Mary, Mary and William. Annaleigh wouldn't wait for them to ask for help anymore. She'd give it to them, whether they wanted it or not.

"It's not a happy birthday, William," Annaleigh said. "It's a miserable one. My two friends—the only friends I have—left me without so much as an explanation. Without a goodbye."

"Goodbye?"

"Are you asking or telling me 'goodbye'?" Annaleigh recrossed her arms, tapped her foot. "And where the hell is Mary?"

Samuel's eyes widened in surprise at her language, her temper.

"She's at our aunt's for the week."

"Oh," she said. She stopped tapping her foot. "No one told me she had gone. No one's told me *anything*."

Carefully, William descended the stairs. He moved so slowly that she thought he might change his mind halfway down and run back to his room. But to her surprise, he didn't. "My father left. He's not coming back."

Annaleigh dropped her arms. "I heard. But not from you." Her voice softened. "You should have told me."

He nodded, watched his feet. "My mother died."

"I know," she said gently.

She remembered the day vividly.

Spring. The air smelled like sugar and honey and the weather was all too perfect for something so terrible. William had promised her the day before that he'd meet her by the lake just before sunset, but he was late, which wasn't unusual.

Annaleigh had begun thinking he wouldn't show up and was readying a speech to deliver to him in her firmest tone. Just when she was abandoning all hope that he was coming, he made his way through the trees. She pulled her feet from the cool water, gathered her words, and then dropped them all.

Her rage drowned in the lake when she saw the look on his face—he was crying. She'd never known him to cry. Not when his father had yelled at him for breaking an antique vase. Not even when he'd broken his arm climbing a tree.

He handed her a letter from his father and she read it to herself. *Your mother has died. I am so very sorry. Please tell Mary that I will be home within the month. George.* Three sentences were all it took to shatter his world.

Annaleigh remembered a certain fury she'd had over the fact that he had signed the terse letter "George" instead of "Father." It was a stupid thing to be upset over, considering the contents of the letter, but it ate at her. It felt so unfamiliar, distant.

It was just the beginning, she later realized, of his removing himself from his children who looked too much like Sara.

She sat with William and held his hand for hours, letting him cry and scream and throw rocks into the lake until the sun rose the next morning. He never mentioned that night again. She didn't bring it up either.

"You didn't apologize…" William said, standing so close to the stairs, as if he didn't want to fully commit to staying so close to Annaleigh. "When you tell people something like that—that their father has left, their mother has died—they apologize." He looked up at her, confused. "It doesn't matter how long ago it happened. A month, a year, a lifetime. There's always an apology. But not from you."

"Of course not." She tucked a loose curl behind her ear, considered him seriously. "Sorries are meaningless when you can't do anything to change the circumstances, William."

And he kissed her. In front of Samuel, next to the open front door, in the early afternoon. His kiss tasted of tears and felt like grief seeking escape, and she returned warm love—an affection that had lived just under her skin for a while but she'd always been too afraid to name it. This was William, her friend. But he was so much more.

He was *her William*.

It was the first time she had been kissed, the first time he had kissed someone and meant it. It was the first time they had found perfect.

Every time she crossed the threshold of the front door to the Calloways' home, she relived that kiss. She didn't know it, but William did too.

Every now and then, when Mary would walk through the house in the late hours of the night, she could still see the scene play out. Two younger shadows of William and Annaleigh framed by the doorway, leaning in for a first kiss over and over again—the energies of the memory living in that one moment forever.

CHAPTER 4

A Promise

MARY WAS IN THE PARLOR standing on a rickety chair next to the fireplace, decorating the tree with giant gold and red globed ornaments when William and Annaleigh returned from the lake. Samuel and the rest of the staff had been given the Christmas weekend off to visit family, so the house was full of echoes and shadows—all except the front parlor, of course. It was the only room in the entire house with any lights on.

"Take your shoes off at the door!" Mary yelled, noticing their arrival. "I saw some snow down by the lake, and I will hang you on this tree if you track it through the house! The floors will be wet for days…"

"Mary, tempting fate, are you?" William asked as he bent over to unlace his shoes. He watched as she wobbled on the chair, reaching to hang an ornament high up on the tree.

"You don't believe in fate, Will."

He shook his head and helped Annaleigh with her boots and coat. "Then you're just testing your balance?" he asked. "Or the craftsmanship of that chair? It's decades old, Mary. It'll break. You'll fall into the fire and turn to kindling in seconds."

With a noise of protest, she jumped down from the chair, arms crossed over her chest in protest. "Happy?"

"More than," he said, taking Annaleigh's hand to join Mary in the parlor.

Mary was barefoot, but her hair was impeccably placed and she was wearing a stunning rose dress, her cheeks flushed nearly the same color. At sixteen, she looked remarkably like her brother, with dark hair and high cheekbones. But where William was cool and gray, Mary was vividly warm.

She was always glowing, as if she had stolen the stars from the night sky and swallowed them whole, wanting to shine from within. Her eyes were even warmer, like melted amber—the same as her mother's, like Annaleigh had seen in every picture of Sara.

Mary was whip smart and had a sharp tongue with a vulgar vocabulary, which William accused her of picking up from Annaleigh. Who had picked it up from whom was entirely up for debate.

"Anna!" She ran forward and threw her arms around Annaleigh, tearing her from William. The ornament hooks poked at Annaleigh's back painfully.

"Ah—Mary."

"Oops," she said, pulling away. "Will, take these and hang them for me since you won't let me finish. Left side—it's looking a bit sparse."

With only a small eye roll, he took the ornaments from her and placed them in their designated spots on the tree. Mary led Annaleigh over to the couch to warm up by the fire. The two girls reached their fingers toward the flames, letting the cold melt from their bones.

"The tree is beautiful, Mary," Annaleigh said. "It's even better than last year's."

"I know! Everything has to be perfect this Christmas." A sly grin lifted one corner of her mouth and she did a terrible job at hiding it. "The gifts are all wrapped, too. I think this is the first year Will's ever placed anything below the tree before Christmas Eve. He's an entire day early."

Annaleigh laughed. "Very unlike him."

"Who knows what other un-Will behavior he'll show next. Maybe he'll bake for us, fold his linens," Mary teased. She tilted her head to the side and raised her chin. "Perhaps we could even—" Her words evaporated, her smile dropping as her eyes widened at Annaleigh. "Will?" She stood up.

"Here it comes," he said from beside the tree.

"What?" Annaleigh looked at him.

"William! You bastard!"

"What a mouth my sister has. Such ugly words from such a pretty girl."

"Is it Christmas Eve?" Mary's voice rose in its pitch. "Because I see a gift that was only supposed to be opened on Christmas Eve, *William*."

"Stop saying my name, *Mary*. It's unsettling."

"This was not the plan," Mary said, her ears reddening with annoyance. "Did you use the sonnet I gave you?"

Oh. Annaleigh's fingers found the locket hanging just under her collarbone. She hadn't remembered she was wearing it— already accustomed to its weight. It was warm in her fingers; it felt alive, resting over her heart.

"Mary—"

She held up a finger, silencing her. "Will, did you use the sonnet?" Silence. "Did you *forget* the sonnet?"

"No, I didn't forget it. I chose not to use it."

"You... you what?"

"Mary," Annaleigh tried again. "It's my fault. I opened it before he could stop me, I didn't know—"

"Do you know how much time I spent finding that sonnet, William? You could have at least recited one single line!"

"Mary," Annaleigh said, touching her arm to get her attention. "We're going to be sisters. I said yes."

She looked back at William, eyebrows raised. "She said yes? No sonnet, and she said yes?"

A nod. "She did."

"To *marry* you?" Mary clarified.

"No, to open a steel mill factory with me. Of course, to marry me!"

"You're sure she said yes?"

"I'm sitting right here, Mary," Annaleigh said. "Ask me yourself!"

"No, no no... I want to hear him say it." She took another step toward William, carefully, slowly, as if she were worried she'd shatter the moment, as if she thought they were all made of glass. "You asked her to marry you, and she said yes?"

"She did," he said. "Actually, I don't think 'yes' was the exact word she used, but—"

Mary rushed at him, hurdling over the back of the couch across from where Annaleigh was sitting, her skirts rustling loudly with her movement. She grabbed his arm, ready to shake him senseless. "Then what was the exact word she used, if not 'yes'? Was it 'no'? Will, I swear on all that is holy, if it was no, I will strangle you."

"'For today, tomorrow, and the rest that follow,'" Annaleigh answered from the couch, eyes locked on William. "'In this life and the next.'"

"Oh." Mary faced her brother. "Well that is much better than a yes."

"It is," he agreed, smiling and watching Annaleigh over Mary's stacked curls.

"You are going to marry him?" Mary looked over her shoulder at Annaleigh, as if she were not quite trusting the truth in their answer, worried that this could be another prank or joke gone too far. "You promise?"

"Honestly, Mary—"

"I promise," Annaleigh answered, her voice strong and clear.

Mary turned back to William and smacked him hard. "Next time I give you a sonnet to use, you *use the damned sonnet*. You could have cost me a sister." It took her a moment to truly register what had happened; calling Annaleigh her *sister* must have triggered something, for Mary's scolding turned immediately into celebration. "You're getting married... You're getting *married*!"

"I'm getting married," he repeated.

They hugged, and for the first time in a very long time, the Calloway siblings seemed truly happy. The ghosts of the past stood back and observed quietly from the shadows the light of the fire they couldn't reach, not daring to intrude on their moment of shared bliss. Their broken family was finally being repaired.

"Me too!" Annaleigh piped up from the couch. "I'm also getting married. Or have you already forgotten?"

Mary squealed and ran back across the room, practically tackling Annaleigh on the couch. "I've never had a sister!"

"I know," she said, laughing. "I've never had a younger sister."

"Thank you," Mary whispered quietly enough that William couldn't hear. "Thank you for marrying my brother. Thank you for loving him."

CHAPTER 5

A Production

UNLIKE THE QUIET CHRISTMAS WILLIAM, Annaleigh, and Mary had spent together, New Year's was loud and filled with guests. For the past two years, the Calloways had played host to ring in the new year in the grandest fashion. Everyone in town was always invited, and often, everyone in town showed up, dressed in decadent gowns and flawlessly tailored suits.

The night always started with pleasantries and propriety but ended in laughter, wrinkled clothing, crushed crinoline, and a scandalous new story made possible by champagne.

Last year, Ava Ailey, a girl about Mary's age who sold flowers in the market, had ended up dancing on a table and singing grossly out of tune. Everyone loved it. The year before that, Mr. Holloway, a banker, had slid down the banister in nothing but his undershirt and trousers. He never did find his shoes.

New Year's was the one time corseted, buttoned-up behavior could be loosened to allow some fun. After all, if the entire town was drunk, there was no one to look down their noses and soberly judge behavior.

This year, Mary had chosen to theme the party as a masquerade. Annaleigh had been excited about it since the announcement had been made and the invitations addressed and sent out back in November. William was never particularly enthused to have so many people over, but he'd played along and tried on every mask Annaleigh had brought him. She'd thought she had found the perfect one—a dark-gray piece that was smooth and reflective. It was beautifully crafted and made his eyes look even stormier than normal, but he hadn't liked the way it molded to his forehead, complaining it was uncomfortable.

The morning of the party, she had brought him a lighter mask that stopped at his eyebrows but covered his cheeks entirely. It looked like it was made from liquid silver, and she imagined rivers of the universe spread across his brows. She was just about to tie it on him when Mary shooed her away.

"Oh no you don't, Anna," she scolded her, snatching the mask away from her before William had a chance to wear it. "The whole point of a masquerade is to have some mystery. Where's the fun in knowing what mask Will's wearing beforehand?"

"I'm sure I'll be able to find him, regardless—"

William's eyes sparked with danger again and a smirk dimpled his cheeks. It was a smile that could only mean trouble. "No, Mary's right. *Mystery, mystique.* I won't know what you will be wearing until I see you for the first time, and you won't know what I'll wear." He stepped toward her, his eyes tracing her neck up to her lips and finally her eyes. He leaned in close and whispered, "I want you to find me."

"Settled, then," Mary said, clapping her hands together. "Will, your mask is sitting in a box under your bed, along with your suit."

He backed out of the room with a quiet laugh and a small wave. "See you tonight."

Mary noticed William cast two shadows as he walked down the hallway, but she said nothing.

At seven, the guests began arriving. Annaleigh was in Mary's bedroom on the second floor, sitting in front of a mirror, being fussed over.

Unnecessarily fussed over, Annaleigh thought. But parties were one of Mary's favorite things, and she didn't mind playing the part of a doll for an hour or so while she primed her with makeup, pinned up her hair, and tightened her corset for her. She really couldn't complain; after Mary was finished with her, she always looked beautiful—almost unrecognizable.

The noise from downstairs started hushed and timid but slowly grew louder and more boisterous as guests continued to arrive. Annaleigh could hear William's laughter rise above the rest, and she started to fidget, wishing to join him.

"We're late to our own party, Mary," Annaleigh said, wincing as a pin jabbed her in the back of the head.

"By design, of course. It's entirely unfashionable to show up precisely when a party begins. Especially for a lady. We're to make a grand entrance. As the last to arrive, all eyes will be on us. It's Will's duty to greet guests as they arrive, not ours." She stepped back and gave Annaleigh's hair a once-over, pursing her lips. With a nod, she turned to her jewelry box and pulled out a glittering comb that she then slid carefully into place, right at the crown of Annaleigh's head. "*Perfect*."

"Mary, it's too much."

"No, it's perfect," she corrected. "Subtle, shiny. Plus, it will hold your wild hair in place for the entire evening! And I like it, which is reason enough." Mary gave a catlike smile, a devious look that said it was not up for debate. "It completes the look just perfectly. All eyes will be on you—and that ring, of course." She took Annaleigh's hand and studied the ring for a moment, sighing.

"Will drew about fifty pictures before he came to this one. I suggested it match the necklace." Mary's eyes flicked to the pendant, but only briefly before returning to the mirror, staring at something just behind them. "My mother would be so happy to have you as a daughter. She would have loved you so much."

Annaleigh smiled, studying the pendant in the mirror. She wished she had had a chance to meet Sara. "None of this feels real. William and I are engaged to be married, and I can't shake the feeling that this is all a dream I'll wake from one day." She found Mary's gaze in their reflection, pulling her attention back from whatever she had been looking at behind them. "What if you're just a dream?"

"Then you should feel privileged. I don't let just anyone dream about me," she joked. "But it's not a dream."

"How do you know?"

Mary moved behind her, wrapped the ties of Annaleigh's corset around her hands, and pulled. Once, twice, three times, crushing all of the air out of her lungs. "Because"—she pulled tighter, knotting the laces together in a tiny bow—"who would wear corsets in their dreams? Can you breathe?"

"Barely."

"Good. Now tie mine."

The girls traded places, Annaleigh moving behind Mary to secure her corset. "Tell me when to stop."

"Stop when you hear my ribs break."

Annaleigh stitched Mary into her corset as tightly as she could, the laces burning her hands the harder she pulled. She could see her ribs bending beneath the pressure of the whalebones, her waist narrowing. Just before she was sure her bones might actually break from the tension, she said, "Finished."

Mary stood and twirled around in front of the mirror. "Beauty is pain, Annaleigh. But it's well worth it."

"I think that may be up for some debate."

The girls stood side by side in the mirror in their underclothes, hair finished and makeup applied. They were nearly the same height but so different in all other appearance.

With her blond hair, Annaleigh should have been the one described as bright and glowing, but she looked pale and lifeless next to Mary's vivid complexion. Together, they looked like an unfinished painting, the artist too lazy to complete the intricate detail of their gowns.

"Sisters," Mary said, smiling. "We even look it. Except for our hair, of course. I wish I were blond. It would make me so much more interesting."

"It's a hair color," Annaleigh said. "Doesn't make you any more or less interesting."

"But it could."

"You're interesting enough as it is!"

She laughed. "You should see me fully dressed. Speaking of which..." Unhooking her arm from Annaleigh's, she crossed to the wardrobe and threw open the wooden doors. Inside hung two ball gowns, one an icy blue, the other a deep violet. "The blue one is yours. The moment I saw it, I knew it belonged to you. I hope you don't mind that I changed your order... I know you wanted the gold one, but this—"

"Is so much better," Annaleigh said, nodding.

Mary beamed. "I knew you'd love it! And when Will sees you in it, he'll fall in love all over again. You know, blue is his favorite color on you."

"It is?"

"Oh yes. Brings out your eyes, adds rosiness to your cheeks." Again, her eyes lost focus, staring at a spot just over Annaleigh's shoulder, just as she had when they were in front of the mirror together. "You never look more alive than when you're in blue."

Annaleigh looked back, expecting to see someone waiting by the bedroom door. She could have sworn she'd felt someone standing there behind her, maybe one of the maids with the shoes Mary had asked her to deliver. For a moment, she thought she had seen a shadow moving quickly past, but when she looked again, there was no one there, only an empty hallway. Still, she could feel eyes on her. A small chill danced its way up her spine.

"Well don't just stand there!" Mary said. "Come try it on!"

Shaking off the sudden coldness she felt, Annaleigh crossed the room to the dresses. They were even more stunning up close. Hers was a faint blue that seemed to shimmer in the light. It was like there was a thin coating of ice or snow dusting the fabric, like it had been dipped in water and clung to its sheen. The skirt was full and ornate, with delicate overlays of spindly flowers. The neck was low and wide, and she knew it would fit her divinely, hugging her gently and exposing her bare shoulders.

William will be very distracted tonight, she thought. Even better, with the neckline what it was, the locket would be the center of attention. She had purposefully put on no other jewelry with exactly that intention.

Mary's dress was so very different from her own but equally as remarkable. It was the deepest shade of violet, the color of the darkest hour of twilight. Black lace around the torso dripped down the skirt and over the bustle in the most beautiful way. In this dress, Mary was sure to look otherworldly. Suddenly, she couldn't wait to see her in it, to try on her own dress.

She removed both dresses from the wardrobe and handed Mary's to her. "Put yours on, too. Then we'll lace each other up again."

Mary snatched her dress and pressed it to her body, spinning in a small, chaotic waltz, finding her reflection turn after turn in the mirror. "They're exactly as I saw them in my mind."

Quickly, the girls dressed and secured one another in the gowns. The measurements were just right—not too tight or too loose, too long or too short. But better than the fit of the gowns was the incredible impact they had on their complexion.

The blue *did* make Annaleigh look vibrant with life. She did not look wan or washed away as she often worried she did with her pale skin. The color reflected on her and contrasted with the rosy flush to her cheeks and shoulders. Her eyes seemed brighter, more startling and intense. And Mary—Mary was the most arrestingly beautiful girl Annaleigh had ever seen.

The dark fabric of her dress added an edge of danger to her look that her brother had always possessed but seemed to evade her; it was an alluring danger, like wanting to run your fingers through the flame of a candle. Her eyes became darker, more gold than brown, and her lips looked as red as blood. Every boy would want to dance with her. Every boy would fall in love with her.

"Oh, wait!" Mary quickly turned Annaleigh away from the mirror. "You can't look at yourself until you're finished!" She ran over to her bed and pulled out two items bundled in parchment. Setting them on her pillow, she tore open the paper and unwrapped two masks.

One was black and trimmed with lace, a large, dark feather affixed to the left side. Obviously that was Mary's, and it would suit her dress magnificently and probably only make her eyes deeper and more gold. The other mask was the same pale blue as

33

her dress. It was narrow, with winged corners at the temple. The ribbon was a soft cream. It was simple, it was lovely, and it was exactly the mask she would have picked out for herself.

"Mary, it's spectacular. Have you been eavesdropping in my dreams? It's like this mask was pulled right from a vision."

Mary's eyes widened, startled, but when Annaleigh laughed, she joined her. She set her mask down and moved to Annaleigh, walking around her to tie together the silky ribbons and secure the mask. It rested gently on her cheekbones, cool and light.

"*Now* you can look," Mary said, turning her around to the mirror.

CHAPTER 6

A Celebration

MUSIC AND LAUGHTER CLIMBED THE staircase and filled the empty spaces in the hallway next to Annaleigh. She paced in the strange shadows cast from the light downstairs, suddenly nervous. New Year's always brought an anxiousness with it for Annaleigh, but this year was different—everything in her life would change. It would be the best change she could have imagined, but it still made her jittery. There was so much good on the horizon that she couldn't help but feel like something terrible was tiptoeing up behind her.

A brittle whisper breathed, tickling the hair that had come undone at the base of her neck. *Too soon.*

A hand set on her shoulder, and Annaleigh spun around only to be greeted by darkness. She searched around herself, assuming she had brushed against a painting on the wall during her pacing, but everything was as it had been before; nothing was askew. The shadows grew darker and colder, but the eerie feeling immediately lifted as Mary came whirling out of her bedroom, mask tied perfectly in place.

"Time to celebrate," she said. She kissed Annaleigh on the cheek and pulled back with a smile that quickly fell when she took in her expression. "What's wrong?"

"Nothing, I just thought—" She stopped, shook her head. "Nothing."

Mary scrunched her nose up in disbelief but said nothing. With a furtive glance and nod to the darkened corridor behind Annaleigh, she reached out and took her arm. "Let's hurry. Will's waiting."

Together, they rushed down the hallway, following the noise of violins and clinking glasses. Mary made her descent down the sweeping stairs first, allowing Annaleigh a moment to stand at the banister and take in the party.

There were *so many people*. She knew that everyone would be there—people she was acquainted with by name or appearance. But tonight, everyone was a stranger to her, all disguised under ornate masks, their eyes shining through in wonder and excitement. A masquerade was just the kind of excitement the town needed.

Looking at all of the guests, Annaleigh searched for William. There were a handful of men who could be him—tall with dark hair—but they all laughed too openly, moved too clumsily. Taking as deep of a breath as she could in her corset, she adjusted her mask on her cheeks to make sure it wouldn't fall off and made her way into to the foyer.

She seemed to float down the stairs, as graceful and pale as an apparition. Slowly, the attention of the guest flickered over to her, small groups hushing to whispers. She searched the crowd for William again, waiting for dark and stormy eyes to meet hers, but by the time she reached the bottom of the staircase, she still hadn't found him.

A man stepped up to her to take her hand as it left the railing. He was stocky with ruddy cheeks and silver hair.

"Annaleigh, you look beautiful." He pulled her close and kissed her cheek.

"Thank you, Father. I'm so glad you could make it."

He lifted his mask off his face to wink at her, a red line from its pressure denting his round cheeks. "Wouldn't miss it. I was told I had to come and see you in your dress. I was promised it would be quite the sight."

Annaleigh rolled her eyes. "Mary?"

Her father laughed. "Your mother's talking to her now," he said, jutting his chin toward the two.

They were huddled close, holding flutes of champagne, grins electrified and conspiratorial. She could only imagine the plans they were making with regard to her wedding, her mother as eager as Mary to see her last daughter married off.

"Have you seen William?" she asked.

"Oh, yes. But I've been sworn to secrecy," he said with a laugh.

"Mary again?" Annaleigh looked over at her and caught her eye. Mary smiled broader, her eyes sparking as Annaleigh's mother whispered something into her ear. That kind of glee meant trouble for Annaleigh. "I wonder how many different dresses they'll make me try on in the upcoming weeks," she said with a sigh.

"Never mind that now. Dance with me?"

He didn't leave her time to protest as he pulled her into the parlor and began a careless waltz.

"My little girl is getting married," he said to her as he spun her around, his arm holding her secure in the dance.

"I'm not so little anymore."

"Yes you are," he said.

"Do you think it's a mistake? To get married so young?" Annaleigh asked.

"Absolutely not." His words were just loud enough for her to hear him over the music. He placed a kiss on the top of her head and continued. "I spoke to William. Did you know he came to ask me for your hand? He wanted my blessing!" He laughed loudly. "I told him that my blessing wouldn't mean much to you. You always went your own way."

"What did he say?" She smiled, imagining William's reaction to her father's dismissal.

"He said he wanted it anyway, that it meant something to him, even if it meant nothing to you."

"It didn't mean *nothing*, Father," Annaleigh said.

"I don't mind. I'm glad at least one of my daughters has my stubborn streak." He lifted her up in a spin, and she joined the women in the air, their skirts fanning below them like blooming flowers. When she landed, he pulled her back to him. "He made quite a case for himself. It was impossible for me to say no."

Annaleigh let out a breathy laugh. "You would have said no?"

"Of course not," he said. "I've seen you two together. I don't think your mother has ever looked at me the way you even glance at him. And your sisters—well, they were all older when they were married, but they've never been so in love. Their husbands adore them absolutely, but it's not even half as much as William loves you. No one loves anyone as much as William loves you, I'd wager."

"Thank you, Father," Annaleigh said.

He kissed her on the top of her head once more before he handed her off to another masked man for the next dance.

The night deepened outside the large windows and the moon rose high above the lake as the party went on. Annaleigh was growing tired of dancing with strangers. The hands that reached out to ask for a dance belonged to everybody but William, it seemed. She'd look up, hopeful that it would be him, only to have to hide her disappointment again and again. The mask, at least, was helping with that.

Mary stood in front of the fireplace and called the attention of the room, clinking her glass. Annaleigh noticed several women pursing their lips in distaste over her unladylike behavior as well as a few boys jerking to attention at the sound of her brilliant voice. They watched her with rapt attention, as if what she said might change their understanding of the world. She could say that the sky had caught on fire and they would ask if she preferred it that way or if she wanted them to douse it out.

"It's nearly midnight, so I thought it appropriate to make a toast." She cleared her throat, lifted her glass higher, and beamed at the crowd, always pleased to be the center of attention. "Three hundred and sixty-five days ago, we promised this year to be the best one yet. In many ways, it was. New bonds of friendship were made, new souls entered the world." She smiled at the Warrens and the tiny, bundled baby girl they held between them. "Not to mention the addition of boysenberry pies down at Drummond's Bakery!"

The room split with laughter and Sally Drummond waved sheepishly, blushing violently under her gold mask.

A slender woman with dark hair swept up from her shoulders came to stand next to Annaleigh. The woman nodded to Mary as the speech went on.

"Quite a spirit, that one," the woman said. Her voice was warm and deep. It had a familiar cadence to it, like a song Annaleigh had heard before but couldn't recall.

"Oh, Mary?" Annaleigh turned to the woman, smiling. "She's magnificent, isn't she?"

The woman watched Annaleigh closely from behind her mask. She was wearing a raspberry dress, the fabric so rich and deep it didn't appear real. It was as though she had stepped into the parlor from another world, from another time. She was a shining memory of a woman. There was something about her sudden presence, her stillness, that sent a spark up Annaleigh's spine. It was like standing next to electricity.

"How is William?" the woman asked, turning her face Mary again. She lifted her chin slightly, tipping her head to the side as Annaleigh had so often seen Mary do. A sense of familiarity tickled the back of her mind.

"I wouldn't know. I haven't been able to find him all night," Annaleigh answered. "But I'm sure he's loving watching me search for him in this crowd. He's quite—" She stopped herself, surprised at the ease of conversation. She hadn't meant to say so much about William, but it was easy to let words slip with this woman. Annaleigh turned toward her and tried to identify the face behind the mask. "I'm sorry, I don't think we've been properly introduced. Or if we have, you're a complete mystery to me in your mask. I'm Annaleigh."

"I know." The woman flicked her eyes to Annaleigh. They were a kind honey brown with flecks of startling gray. She had a gaze that felt like a summer storm. Something about her was so achingly familiar, but for the life of her, Annaleigh couldn't pin the thought down. Where ever did she remember her from?

Mary's voice rose above the clamor. "It's been a splendid year, but I can't help but see the shadows of those absent," she continued. "My father, over in England, or our mother—" Her gaze sought out Annaleigh. When she found her, her mouth popped open, the words on her lips temporarily forgotten as she took a quick gasp. Annaleigh hoped her corset wasn't laced too tightly, but before she had to worry, Mary shook her head and went on. "My parents, who I know would have been so thrilled to have entertained you all."

The woman shifted beside Annaleigh, rustling her skirts.

Mary stood on her tiptoes and appeared to be searching the room for someone, holding her breath. When she came up empty, she continued, adding more brightness and excitement into her voice. "But I'll have a new family, and I want to ring in this beautiful new year with a toast to Will and his bride-to-be, Anna."

Now it was Annaleigh's turn to blush. She turned back to the woman but found that she had left. A man in a velvet suit had taken her place instead, and he chortled a boozy, sloppy laugh.

"I have never in my life known two people who love each other more, and I have enjoyed every second of witnessing your detestation grow into infatuation. Anna—you're my best friend, my sister, and my favorite person in the world. Sorry, Will," she said, laughing.

The room joined her. Mary had a glow of happiness that was contagious. A smile from her was mirrored a thousand times by everyone watching. She reflected joy, sparkled with laughter.

She found Annaleigh in the crowd again and held her gaze, her face growing serious. For a moment, fear flickered in and out of her eyes, but it was gone so quickly that no one could be sure it was there at all.

"To this year and the many more that will follow," she said, suddenly rushing to end the speech. "May they be filled with laughter, love, and light. Happy New Year!"

Everyone raised their glasses. "Happy New Year!" they repeated. The room filled with the tinkle of clinking glasses.

"Now how about another dance?" Mary called over the crowd. She waved her hand and the music started up again, a cheery, plucky piece where partners spun and switched hands every time the pace changed.

Annaleigh lost sight of Mary as she was whisked away by a boy in a mossy-green mask. Before she knew it, she too was pulled into the dance. The champagne had made all the lights in the room streaky, shooting like stars across her vision when she twirled from partner to partner. It was a magical effect that lived somewhere between brilliant and blinding. She held tight to her partners to ensure she wouldn't stumble over herself. The music's tempo sped up, and the man in the blue mask became a man in an orange mask who turned into another man with a mask that carved his forehead with flames.

She closed her eyes to try to dispel some of the dizziness, but she opened them again when the next partner took hold of her. Instantly she felt the change, a shift of energy that jolted through her bones and lit lines of gunpowder in her veins.

His hand spread across her lower back, pressing them closer together and impeding her view of him. But she didn't need to see him to know—she'd finally found William.

"You've been hiding from me," she whispered just loud enough for him to hear over the music and the chatter of the party.

"I was not hiding." She could hear the grin in his voice. "I like watching you dance. Though that one with the dragon mask seemed to be enjoying himself a little too much. I had to step in— I could only take so much."

She let her head rest on his chest as he spun her to the edge of the dance floor. "You should have come to me earlier."

"Where's the fun in that?"

"We could have danced more. You could have saved me from at least a dozen dull conversations!"

The music died as everyone bowed and clapped, gathering around a tall grandfather clock in the foyer. They began counting down to midnight, loud and drunk.

Annaleigh went to join, but William held on to her hand and pulled her back to him.

"This way," he said, leading her through a few shadowy rooms.

In the dark, they stumbled and collided with the kitchen counter, sending pots crashing to the floor, but William didn't slow his pace until they pushed out of the stuffy house and into the cool night air. The harsh chill of winter had ebbed away for the night, allowing a comfortable cold to replace the heat and flush Annaleigh had felt after dancing for hours.

The sky was impossibly clear, the stars so bright that the gas lamps hadn't needed to be lit for the yard to be in perfect clarity.

"Beautiful," she found herself whispering.

"I couldn't agree more," William said, but when she turned to face him, she found that he wasn't watching the night's sky. Behind his onyx mask, his eyes were drinking her in instead, not even mildly interested in the infinity of stars that coiled and swirled above them.

He traced her dress with his eyes only seconds before his hands followed suit, fingers inching up from her waist to her hips and ribs. Carefully, he brushed her collarbone, smiling as he touched the chain of the locket.

"You've been so distracting all night. I was half tempted to rush to you the instant I saw you on the staircase. It took everything in me to hold still."

Annaleigh shivered, goose bumps rising on her arms— though whether they were from the late December air or William's touch, she wasn't sure.

"Are you cold?" he asked, unbuttoning his suit jacket to give to her.

She stopped his hands and shook her head. "Quite flushed, actually. Are you cold?"

He moved his hands back to her waist, eyes darkening. "The exact opposite."

Voices drifted out to them. *"Ten! Nine! Eight! Seven!"*

William leaned in, pulling Annaleigh into his arms. They stumbled backward until her back pressed up against a column

43

of the balcony, cold and solid behind her. She was glad for its support; she needed something to steady her, to keep her afloat and breathing as she dove heedlessly into the ocean that was William. His hands were on her waist, hers in his hair, and their senses tossed to the heavens.

They were night and day living in one impossible moment. William was a shadow pressed close to the figment of a girl so pale she had to have been designed by the moonlight. Surely she'd disappear with the dawn.

"Five!"

Time grew lazy, seconds swimming past them so lethargically they seemed to have halted their passage altogether. With one of his hands, William reached behind her and untied the ribbons of her mask as she shoved his over his forehead. They went crashing to the ground together.

"Four!"

Their hearts beat recklessly fast, knocking against each other's chest as if asking to gain entrance. Breathing seemed overrated; Annaleigh was drowning on dry land, but it was worth it if she could live on his lips forever.

His mouth moved to the hollow in her throat, following her pulse down to her collarbone until he stilled, hovering just above her heart.

"Three! Two!"

In the cold, their rushed breaths fogged together, though neither noticed.

"One!"

He collapsed into her, incoherent and desperate, tracing the path he had taken to her heart back up again until he landed on her lips. The kiss was sweet with champagne.

This is what it is like to kiss the stars, Annaleigh thought. *This is what it's like to taste the universe.*

She wasn't sure how much time had passed, but when they finally parted, the noise of the party had died down to a distant hum.

William leaned forward, resting his forehead on hers. "Did I tell you how incredible you look tonight?"

"Not yet," she said, smiling to herself.

"There are no words—beautiful is too insignificant a descriptor for you. It's too small to encompass all that you are." A beat of silence passed between them. "Blue is my favorite color on you."

She closed her eyes. "I know. Mary told me. It's why she picked this dress."

"You look like winter itself. A frozen angel, so incredibly radiant." He lifted his hand to her face, his thumb sliding over her cheek, just below where her mask had been. "I want to marry you."

"You will."

"*Now.*"

She placed her hand on his heart, felt its insistent, impatient thundering. The storm in his eyes had moved to his chest. "Soon."

"It won't be soon enough. It will never be soon enough," he said, whispering. "I want all of you, forever, starting now. I don't want to wait any longer. I think I'll go mad."

Gently, she kissed him. "Fine."

"Fine?"

"Yes. Let's get married as soon as possible."

He lifted her up, spinning her away from the column. The skirts of her dress fanned out wide, murmuring softly together. When he set her down, he kissed her again. It was a kiss of surrender. He gave her everything he had, pouring every last ounce of emotion—his love, his joy, his fear—into her. She tightened her hold on him, pulling him closer, and handed him her heart in return.

As they kissed, the moon watched in wonder, and she could have sworn she had heard a whisper, soft with concern.

My son, my son.

CHAPTER 7

A Change of Plans

IN THE MORNING, AFTER THE last of the celebration stragglers had found their way out of the great house and back down into town, William and Annaleigh found Mary to tell her that they wanted to move up their wedding date. The news, unsurprisingly, incensed Mary, and she grew impressively loud for someone who claimed to be hung over with a throbbing headache. While she yelled at them, her breath still smelled like flat champagne, stale from sleep.

"First you move the proposal up, and now you decide to change the date from the summer to just a few weeks away?" Mary's hair was down from its pins, dark ringlets bouncing with every wild gesture she made. "Six months you endeavor to steal from me! I have appointments set, dresses ordered to be *custom fitted*. Flowers were to be sent over from Paris—flowers that will not bloom until late spring! I cannot control the seasons, William, and I will not be able to find the flowers I want in the dead of winter! Unless the cold recedes early, Annaleigh won't even have a decent bouquet." She crossed her arms, punctuating her annoyance at the idea of a flowerless ceremony. "There is so much to do! Things simply cannot happen overnight!"

Annaleigh sat on William's bed, watching him try to chase his sister around the room to settle her down. She would have felt guilty for complicating Mary's plans if it weren't so humorous to listen to her list everything that needed alterations, and William did not seem to understand a word she was saying. There was a reason Mary planned every party herself.

"We do not need all of this, Mary. Annaleigh and I—we do not wish for some grand ceremony. We don't need strangers to watch on as we are married. It can be small, simple. Just us."

Mary looked at Annaleigh. "Anna, is this true?"

She nodded. "Really, we don't need much."

"Who will be there, then?"

William listed the guests on his fingers, Mary's face falling into mortification with every name. "Annaleigh's mother and father. An invitation should be sent to her sisters and their husbands, though I doubt they will be able to make it. Our father, if he cares to show up. Samuel and the girls who work around the house as they've practically raised us. And you."

The fact that the guest list could be counted on his fingers was enough to throw Mary into another fit.

"That's it?" Her eyes widened so greatly Annaleigh was sure they would roll out of her head. "Less than ten people in total?"

"Why not?"

With a dramatic eye roll, she fell on the bed next to Annaleigh. "I am not even sure where to begin answering that question…"

Annaleigh lay back on the bed, her shoulder bumping Mary's. "Please, Mary? Something uncomplicated. I cannot wait any longer. Six months of engagement would be torturous. Surely you can understand?"

The floorboards creaked as William crossed the room to stand at the foot of the bed, watching her. His eyes found Annaleigh's and they darkened, taking on the deep color they were on New Year's Eve. Her cheeks flushed, remembering his hands on her body as one year had slipped into the next, unnoticed in their shared moment.

Unexpectedly, Mary sat up, hand to her mouth, hiding a smile. She looked at Annaleigh, touching her arm as if confirming she were real. She whispered a few quick, quiet words to herself—something about flowers and frost. Then she grinned a smug smile that dimpled her cheeks and wrinkled her nose. Her hair was disheveled and framed her face so haphazardly that she looked insane.

"Fine. I cannot move it up to January—there's too much to do for that to be even slightly feasible. But the first Saturday of February… That could be possible."

"February it is," Annaleigh said.

"Isn't that—" William began, but Mary cut him off.

"The date Mother and Father married? Yes." She watched him, challenging him to change his mind, to get married in May or June like he had planned. But when he remained silent, she knew she had won.

The memory of his mother would be ever-present on the day of their marriage; it was a pain he would have to address eventually. Perhaps it would hurt less on a day filled with such joy.

"It will be perfect," Mary said. "Mother will love—" She stopped, her words silently falling from her open mouth as she glanced out to the hallway as if something had caught her attention. With a soft smile, she closed her mouth and looked at William again, no more challenge in her eyes. "Settled, then. February second."

Pulling his hand over his face in resignation, William repeated, "February second."

Luck was on their side—or Mary's side, at least. The snowy winter had dissipated into unseasonably warm temperatures, and the florist finally had some flowers for Mary to arrange. They still had to be sent out for, of course, but Mary found a beautiful selection miles south where flowers were just beginning to consider blooming.

Every day of January was busy, packed with appointments for Annaleigh and assignments for William. Mondays were dedicated to finding an orchestra, food, and seating for the entire town (the first of many compromises Mary was able to convince them of).

Tuesdays were for writing invitations and working on penmanship, a particular weakness of William's.

"*February* second, Will," Mary would scold him. "Throw that invitation away. If anyone receives it, they'll have no idea what the date is! Write slower…"

Wednesdays were for fittings. Somehow, Mary had still managed to find a dressmaker to design a custom wedding gown for Annaleigh. So every Wednesday, no matter how little sleep she'd gotten the night before, Annaleigh would stand for hours on a pedestal while an elderly woman who spoke clipped French rapidly to Mary measured and pinned bolts of fabric and lace to her.

Every Thursday, William would leave the house for the day, traveling to neighboring towns and cities looking for more expensive, unique items Mary had ordered.

On Fridays, Annaleigh's mother would visit, and she and Mary would sit on the floor, going through the mess of plans they had made that week. Rolls of fabrics in every different shade of cream and white were scattered across the floor, invitation samples were embossed and stacked on top of books filled with poems and Bible verses, and parchment with rough sketches of the ceremony setup were passed between the two. Some were crumpled and tossed into the fire, while others were placed up on the couch for further consideration.

"Those are possibilities." Annaleigh's mother nodded in approval one Friday afternoon. "Though it might be claustrophobic to have the ceremony in here. A party is one thing—dancing, standing. With the couches out of the way, there's quite a bit of room. But with this many individual chairs and an aisle…" She pursed her lips. "Are you sure you won't have it in a church, Anna?"

She and Mary peeked their heads over the couch to look for Annaleigh, who was usually hiding somewhere in the kitchen or study, smuggling time for some light reading not related to weddings.

"No church," she called back, her voice echoing in the empty space between them. "That's only important to you, Mother. Not me."

"Anna, come in here for a moment!" Mary called after another hour of debating.

Begrudgingly, she snapped her book closed and made her way back into the parlor.

"What if…" Mary's eyes sparkled, excitement boiling just under the surface.

She tried to control her voice, to seem less thrilled by her idea so she could sell it well, but her bluffs were as bad as her brother's. This was a family that could not lie to save their lives.

"We could have it in the center of town?" Her voice tripped up like it was more a question than a statement. "Think about how grand that would be. Flowers in every window, candles, under the stars… It would be beautiful!"

"Too ostentatious, Mary. Think smaller, more personal."

"Well what do *you* have in mind?"

A small voice in the back of her head gave her an idea. "We could have it by the lake."

She had meant it only as a suggestion, an idea she knew would be shot down, but as soon as she said it aloud, all other options went out of her head. *It has to be the lake.*

"There's certainly enough room. You and William met there," her mother said, considering. "Didn't you?"

"When they were swimming..." Mary said distantly, her eyebrows pulled together. "That's what he told me, anyway."

Annaleigh nodded, memories flooding her thoughts. The lake was the first place she'd seen him, where she'd first argued with him. It was where he'd told her about his mother dying, where they'd shared secrets, wishes, and dreams. There were so many nights they'd spent together down at the lake. Summers swimming, winters ice skating... They'd climbed trees together, skipped rocks, and sent tiny paper boats sailing over the smooth surface.

They shared their second kiss at the lake. It wasn't as dramatic as their first kiss, which had begun with yelling. This was a different kind of kiss—a kiss that was patient and careful, slow and burning.

It was a few weeks after their first kiss. Enough time had passed that Annaleigh wondered if he'd ever kiss her again or if he regretted kissing her at all. They were lying under the stars. The nights had just started getting cold, the summer stealing away every evening to let fall creep closer. She remembered being freezing that night, her hair still wet from swimming earlier that afternoon. Her teeth were chattering so loudly that the crickets around them had gone quiet. William offered to go home and bring her a coat or a quilt, but she told him she wasn't cold; she wasn't ready for him to leave yet.

"And you think *I'm* a bad liar," he said, laughing.

"I'm not cold!" she protested, putting power in her voice as if she could will it to be true.

Without correcting her, or calling her out on her second lie, William found her hand in the dark. Her chattering teeth stopped. The muscles in her legs stopped twitching. Her body stopped fighting the cold as his warm hand enveloped her icy one.

"The stars are…"

"I know," he said.

He shifted so he was closer to her, so the full length of their bodies touched and bounced heat back and forth. There was a heavy breath of silence before he spoke again as he took a moment to gather his courage.

"They remind me…of your eyes," he said. "Every time I look up at night, I see you watching me back."

"No," she said, blushing in the dark. "It was beautiful." And she leaned over to kiss him.

Almost a year after that kiss, he told her he loved her. And the lake was also where he had accidentally proposed to her. She wondered now if he would have proposed there if he had had the choice, if he had planned it to be there anyway.

There were a lot of memories next to the lake. She wanted to make a new one.

"No," Mary said suddenly, breaking Annaleigh out of her memories. "Not the lake. That… It just won't work."

"Well, it could," Annaleigh's mother pointed out, pulling a journal to her lap, "if we went with this layout that you drew. In fact, it would work out quite well. Much more room to set up. Of course, there are many other issues, like the weather."

"It won't work," Mary said again. "The weather, all that sand, the mud… There's a lot that could go wrong. It's a bad idea."

"Mary, it's the best idea!" Annaleigh insisted. "Please? If you let me have it at the lake, I promise I'll stop complaining at the dress fittings. You can decide everything else!"

"Annaleigh—"

"Mary," Annaleigh mimicked back.

The front door opened and closed loudly, breaking the tension between the two. Annaleigh looked up to see William handing off his coat to Samuel. He smiled when he saw her watching him. For the ghost of a second, she thought she could see his mother standing at the bottom of the stairs, like she might have done many years ago. But as William moved across the foyer, the image disappeared, like dust blown away.

"The lake," Annaleigh said to Mary again, more confidently. "We would love it to be at the lake. Wouldn't we, William?"

He looked up at her and quirked his eyebrows, obviously sensing the danger of interjecting himself into whatever argument he had walked in on.

Her mother laughed darkly. "You better pray the snow does not return. A storm would be the one thing that could ruin this day."

Mary tipped her head, considering. After a moment, her frown deepened, her lips forming silent words as she wrote something down. Her fingers tapped nervously on her lap as she squeezed her eyes closed and shook her head.

"It will be fine, Mother," Annaleigh assured her. "It would take much more than snow to kill the day."

With a humming sound, Mary stood up and left the room, brushing quickly by William as she ran up the stairs.

"What happened here?" he asked, moving into the room.

Annaleigh's mother shrugged. "Must be feeling ill. We have had to finalize all of our plans today." She set down the stack of papers she was shuffling. "Just one more week."

William came over to Annaleigh, taking her in his arms. He brushed a kiss across her forehead and whispered, "Still not soon enough."

Part 2

I was a child and she was a child,
In this kingdom by the sea,
But we loved with a love that was more than love —
I and my Annabel Lee —
With a love that the wingèd seraphs of Heaven
Coveted her and me.

— Stanza II, *Annabel Lee* by Edgar Allan Poe

CHAPTER 8

The Morning

SATURDAY'S SUNRISE SPILLED PINK ACROSS the lake. Annaleigh, unable to fall back asleep, watched the early morning brighten and shift through the warm colors of waking.

The guest room Mary had set up for her last fall was cool and silent. As Annaleigh stood looking out the window, she couldn't keep her mind on the present, and she was much too nervous to even begin to consider the future. It was an excited bundle of anxiety, but it still made her stomach drop and her head spin. *This afternoon, she would be married.*

This early, the house was still quiet. There was only the slight shifting groan of floorboards, the whisper and hiss of bed sheets being tossed around in Mary's room as she had another fitful sleep. She'd been having a lot of those lately, probably due to the odd hours she kept, staying up all night planning, ensuring that every last detail would be perfect. Some nights, Annaleigh could hear her talking to herself. It always sounded like arguing, but she could never make out any specific words through the walls.

With one last look out the window to the lake and woods below, Annaleigh left her window to creep from her room and down the hall. She hadn't fully decided to visit William, but before she could stop herself, she eased the door open and tiptoed inside.

Unsurprisingly, he was still asleep. Since she'd known him, he'd slept the same: sprawled across his bed and knotted in blankets with pillows askew. That morning when she found him, he was lying on his stomach, the bed sheets twisted around his legs as if he had been fighting them off all night. His head rested under one of his arms.

She stepped closer, picking a pillow off the ground and whispering his name. "William?"

He stirred but didn't wake, only turned his head toward her voice, further mussing up his unruly hair. She smiled to herself, replaced his pillow, and lay down next to him, curling her hand around his.

She couldn't stop watching him, trying to remember every moment. She had the urge to memorize him now, to study every angle of his face, count the freckles over his cheeks, or touch every patch of scruff on his jaw and kiss across his strong jaw. She wanted to remember him as he was now, asleep and at peace. She felt as if everything would change tonight, and she wanted to be able to notice the differences. The years they'd spent together floated through her memories in just a few stuttering heartbeats.

It felt like she'd met him yesterday, like she'd known him forever.

Annaleigh's nerves melted away when she was this close to William. Perhaps the future wouldn't be as terrifying as she believed. The unknown didn't have to be scary. Possibilities were hopeful—there was so much to live for, so many *maybes* and *what-ifs* that life could be whatever she made it.

Annaleigh didn't need to worry over questions about tomorrow when she had William. As long as they were together, there was nothing to be afraid of. Gently, she pressed her lips to his knuckles and closed her eyes, burrowing closer to her William.

Destiny danced around their entwined bodies, quiet and melancholic.

She hadn't meant to fall asleep. When Annaleigh blinked awake, she immediately sat up, worried about the strict schedule she was meant to keep today. If she was already running late, her mother and Mary would —

A small laugh and a warm hand pulled her back down to the bed. "No one's awake yet."

"You're awake," she pointed out, turning around in William's arms to face him. His chest was warm under her cheek.

"Am I? Feels more like a dream to me."

He kissed her, his fingers tracing patterns up her back and scattering away the last of her sleepiness. Just then, she realized how thin her nightgown was, how insignificant the blanket covering him was. Her cheeks heated for a moment before she threw caution to the wind and damned propriety, pulling him closer and eliciting a low rumble to escape the back of his throat. She didn't care how much he saw of her now, how much he felt—they were getting married today. A few hours made little difference.

William turned over her, his arms braced on either side of her body. He held himself just a breath away. Electricity lived between them, sparking like wildfire between their chests.

Annaleigh was a mess of gold under him, curls crushed beneath her and further undone by his hands as he wove his fingers through her hair.

"You smell like jasmine," he whispered against her, his voice hoarse as he attempted to catch his breath.

"Mary…" she said, her voice hitching. It was hard to concentrate with his hands on her. "Mary put some of the flowers in my room until the ceremony."

He caught her mouth with his again. The kiss was slow and punctuated by the smile he couldn't keep from his face. "Our wedding."

The door to his room swung open, cracking loudly on the wall. Standing with her arms crossed and a stare that sent Annaleigh hiding under the blankets was Mary. "Must I chaperone you two at every moment?" She marched over to the bed and tore off the bed sheets, letting them pile on the floor.

William let out an exasperated sigh and pulled his hand over his face. "I really wish you wouldn't."

"If you would keep your hands to yourself, Will, I wouldn't need to," Mary said, finding Annaleigh's arm and marching her out of the room. "There will be plenty of time for *this* after today. I will not have you messing everything up after I spent so much time planning for today. I will not have you… You won't… It's my *duty* to…" She looked back once, pointed at him, and said in her sternest voice, "You are not to see her until tonight."

"Mary—" they both protested at once.

"It's not up for debate." She gave Annaleigh a slight push and gestured down the hall. "March."

"Mary," William called after her just before she pulled the door closed.

She paused, keeping her eye on Annaleigh to make sure she went back to her own room. "Yes, Will?"

He jumped out of bed and stuck his head out of his room, trying to peek around Mary and the door she held in front of her for one last glimpse of Annaleigh. "Just…tell Anna I love her and that I can't wait until she is my wife."

"I think she knows," Mary said.

"Thank you. For the wedding—for everything. I know it was short notice."

For all their bickering, the two Calloways loved one another more than any other brother and sister. They were each fiercely protective of the other, and their loyalty was strong to a fault. It made them unflinchingly honest with each other, which often led to fights and disagreements over even the simplest things. But they seemed to live for arguing, for poking at one another in a playful way as only siblings could. Beyond their quarrels, though, was an unbreakable allegiance.

"Of course, Will," Mary said. "I really wish you two would have held it somewhere else. The lake is… It would have been better in town."

The picture of the town Mary envisioned, decorated in finery so extravagant that every building appeared lit with magic, would have been much better. The lake was wrong, but she couldn't tell William why, didn't want him to call her crazy. She'd heard that enough as a child when she would tell him about the dreams she'd have about their mother. Dreams that were something *more*.

Mary was anxious about today, but for an entirely different reason than Annaleigh. It felt too cold for a day that was meant to be cheery. She needed everything to be perfect for her brother and Annaleigh, to be exactly as she had seen it. It had to be just right—or everything would go terribly wrong.

Her back prickled, like pins were set into her spine. Something was off. She felt that something had already gone wrong. But she had been so careful. The trees were still bare; the flowers hadn't yet bloomed. This morning, though, was happening exactly as she had seen it last week when they were planning it all. She hadn't been wrong yet.

When she had looked out her window that morning, it had reminded her of the strange dream she'd had the other night — the foggy lake, cold air, painful breaths, and a floating girl, her skin the same shade of blue as Annaleigh's New Year's dress. The dream was broken and nonsensical, images overlapping and shattering apart before she could make any sense of it all. If it was too cold tonight for the ceremony by the lake…

It had to be fine. *No flowers*, she reminded herself. When she had seen it, there had been flowers. *It can't happen today.*

Still not looking at William, she shook her head, trying to dissipate what nightmares followed her into the waking hours, but her thoughts slipped past her mouth before she could stop them.

"Something's wrong," Mary said. She trapped her lip between her teeth before more words rushed out to answer the questioning look he gave her.

"What do you mean?" he asked.

She tipped her head back to study him, wanting to say more, but when she caught the shape of the shadow behind him — the slight shake of a head, warning — she stepped back and smiled. "It's probably nothing. Bad dreams, no sleep, too much tea."

Now it was William's turn to study Mary, to pick out every feature on her face that reminded him so much of their mother. No wonder his father had had to leave them; staring at the face of a ghost every day could drive a man mad.

"You suggested the second of February," William said.

"For mother."

Mary wrung her hands, taking them away from the door. She had never looked so small to William as she did in that moment. He often wondered how she could bear having the memory of their mother so close to the surface, always talking about her, looking at pictures, having imaginary conversations with her as a child… Was it all finally catching up to her? Is that why she looked so shaky, so sick?

"Do you think that's why father isn't coming?"

He shrugged. "I think there are many reasons he did not want to come."

"We can delay it. A week? Maybe two?" she suggested, a note of hope in her voice. "He might not have been able to travel this week, but if we give him more time… I could move the ceremony somewhere nicer. We could travel for it? Maybe he would come if it wasn't here."

"Is that what's wrong?"

No. Maybe. Probably not.

"Nothing is wrong," she said dismissively, waving her hand to prove her point.

Another easy smile slipped back on her face, and she turned away from the room of shadows behind William. Her nightmare could mean nothing. It was true that she wasn't getting enough sleep. The things she saw might not be as accurate when she was this tired. She'd never *been* this tired before.

But I have yet to be wrong, she worried.

"See you tonight, Will," Mary called over her shoulder. "Look handsome."

CHAPTER 9

The Wedding

EVERY SEAT WAS FILLED. ANNALEIGH could see William waiting at the end of the aisle, dressed in his nicest suit. It reminded her of the one he had worn on New Year's, a dark blue so deep it could be the color of the bottom of the lake. It took her breath away.

He was fidgety, which was unlike him, looking out over the water and adjusting his jacket every few seconds.

There was an odd energy to the late afternoon. The crowd stirred, restless, though they'd only just sat down, and Annaleigh, who waited by herself at the edge of the woods, felt crowded. It was as if there were a dozen people waiting behind her, pressing close. There were eyes on her, hands grabbing her. Despite the close, suffocating feeling of being surrounded by bodies, she was alone and very cold. But she could feel the pull on her dress, the sweep of someone's fingers up her spine and down her arm, so distinctly she thought she'd lose her mind.

Nerves, she explained away. *Excitement.*

Mary came running through the grove of trees where she had tucked Annaleigh away and out of sight. "Anna!"

She jumped, her heart in her throat. *"Really*, Mary, are you trying to scare me to death? You're more like your brother than people give you credit for."

"Sorry, sorry," she said quickly, leaning forward and kissing her cheek. She handed her a bouquet of beautiful yellow jasmine with shaking hands. "It's time." Mary twitched at a loose curl that hung over her face, her eyes wide and anxious, and asked one last time, "Are you sure you want to have the ceremony here, at the lake?"

"Mary—"

"No, you're right. Too late for that now." She searched the trees above her and found them bare. Taking a deep breath to try to calm herself, she straightened her hair. "It's okay. We're fine." She smiled and kissed Annaleigh again. "Sorry. Maybe your nerves are rubbing off on me."

Annaleigh let out a shaky laugh.

"Now, let's go get you married to my brother."

The air rushed from her lungs as if someone had tightened her corset. An invisible hand lay against the small of her back, gentle and careful. It was so *real*, but she watched as Mary clapped her hands together in front of her and pressed them to her mouth, swallowing a sob. *Just my imagination.*

"You're beautiful, Anna."

With the hand that wasn't holding the bouquet, Annaleigh reached up and adjusted the pendant of the necklace, making sure it was lying just right. "I think I'm going to be sick. I can't breathe."

Mary's face blanched.

"The corset. I think… I think it's too tight. Mary?"

"Oh…" She shook her head, turned away to compose herself. After taking a few deep breaths and studying the guests of the wedding, she faced Annaleigh again. "Of course, the corset." She moved behind Annaleigh to check the ties and let them out ever so slightly. "Better? You'll be fine." Her hands were shaking, but she kept her voice steady. "You'll be fine."

Annaleigh tried to take a breath, but it still felt like her lungs were being crushed. "I can't breathe. It didn't do any good, Mary..."

Mary put a hand on her shoulder and made her face her. "You can breathe. You're okay. It will go perfectly, because I planned it. Your mother and father are in the first row, and Will is waiting for you at the end of that aisle." She stepped forward and made a few more small adjustments to Annaleigh's hair before stepping back to smile.

"I'm so scared, Mary." There were too many people, too many things to go wrong. What if she tripped? What if she forgot her vows?

But she knew that wasn't what was really scaring her. Her life would change after today. It was the best change she could ask for—but she wasn't used to a happiness like this. She didn't know what to do with it.

"I know, Anna. Me too." Mary reached out and wove their fingers together, squeezing her hand once in her own. "We're all scared, every last one of us. I think that's the secret—no one knows what they're doing. They just pretend, and things work themselves out. For the most part. I think..."

Annaleigh laughed nervously.

"I promise I will be right in front of you, Will right next to you. You'll never be alone. Not ever again."

The thought composed Annaleigh, smoothed away the wrinkles of anxiety that scrunched her forehead. Mary's eyes slid to something just past her shoulder, but Annaleigh didn't bother to turn around and look. It looked like she was seeing something that wasn't there, her eyes cloudy on the present as they focused on an old memory or maybe a wish she had for the future.

The pressure from the invisible hand on her lower back disappeared, and Annaleigh found that she could breathe again. *See? Just nerves.*

She settled the veil around herself and took one last steadying breath. "I'm ready."

Mary made her way down the narrow aisle between the rows of seating that fanned wide around the lake. William looked up as he saw his sister approach, smiling. He looked so handsome and dark with the glassy surface of the water reflecting the sky behind him. He appeared to belong to the sea, to be the waves themselves come to life—reckless and wonderful.

Fate followed Annaleigh as she walked toward destiny, her pace slow and cautious. The veil gave a gauzy, ghostlike appearance to everything. It was unearthly and beautiful, almost like magic. She could feel time slow when her eyes met William's. He took in her dress with an expression somewhere between overwhelming joyfulness and disbelief. It made her heart swell and tears pool precariously in her eyes; it took all she had to keep the bubble of laughter in her chest.

She glanced quickly over the guests who had all come to bear witness to their love. She saw her mother and father huddled close together with rosy cheeks sparkling with tears. Samuel was sitting toward the front near where William stood. He looked as proud as a father watching his son. She saw the empty seat for where William's father should have been, but this time, it didn't cause her anger, only pity that he would miss something so important.

For a gasp of a breath, she thought she saw Mary sitting in the crowd, a few chairs behind Samuel. She looked older, a sad crescent smile turning her lips, and the tears in Annaleigh's eyes made her appear foggy. But when a woman in a large hat shifted forward and back again, attempting to gain a better view of the bride, Mary disappeared. The image of her was replaced by that of an old man with dark hair and a full mustache. She must have imagined it all.

At the end of the grassy aisle of scattered flowers was a great arch. William stepped down to take her hand, and Mary took away the burden of the bouquet.

The ceremony began, but Annaleigh wasn't aware of anything but William, and he only seemed to see her. The voices that spoke around them, reciting whatever her mother had asked the priest to read, were muffled and distant. The sky faded to violet above them, and the world seemed alive with colors. The golden flowers that were laced through Annaleigh's hair and tucked into William's suit, the midnight water of the lake, the green of the grass beneath their feet and the tops of the trees that were just coming back to life... Mary had been wrong—spring was blooming unseasonably early this year. The brilliant shifting tones of twilight made it all bewitchingly enchanting.

When they exchanged vows, neither of them could stop smiling. William and Annaleigh were lost to one another. The crowd had disappeared, allowing them to remain together, the only two in the entire empty world. It all felt like a dream, too impossibly happy to be real.

The rings somehow found their way onto each of their fingers, and before she realized they were at the end, William was lifting her veil, leaning close, and kissing her for the first time as her husband.

Annaleigh closed her eyes and willed time to freeze, for this moment to stretch into infinity. But all too soon, they pulled apart to the sound of cheers.

Dazed, she looked over her family and friends again. Samuel was crying, as were most of the girls from the house. When she looked back at Mary, she found her staring out at something on the lake. She tried to turn to see what she was looking at but only caught a column of mist twisting strangely across the surface of the water. Feeling her gaze, Mary spun around and found Annaleigh's eyes, smiling.

"Sisters," she mouthed, beaming.

"Sisters," Annaleigh repeated back.

Before she could look back over the lake again, William whisked her down the aisle and away from the crowd. Mary stood on the bank of the lake, her heels sinking slightly into the sand as she stared at them.

A voice came from over her shoulder, sounding as insubstantial as the wind. *You must save him.*

"I need to save her first," Mary whispered, watching the guests file out of their seats and follow the path back to the house.

You know the impossibility of that dream. But his life is still in the balance. It's up to you to save him.

"I do not think I will be able to," she answered to no one but the water as the chairs emptied. "Not after this."

CHAPTER 10

The Lake

IT FELT LIKE NEW YEAR'S again. The house was once again brimming with brightly colored dresses and handsome suits. Laughter, music, and the chiming clink of champagne glasses filled the great rooms. Dancing began in the parlor, and every room on the first floor was decorated with flowers and tables of delicate food. It was comfortably crowded—warm and pleasant.

Annaleigh felt jittery with excitement. She couldn't force herself to move away from William's arm. She had the oddest sensation that, the moment she let go, they'd be lost to each other, separated by some invisible force, never to embrace again. It was a foolish, illogical thought, but she didn't want to risk the space.

When others came to congratulate them and shake his hand, she remained at his side, touching his elbow or his back, never allowing an inch of space between them.

Most of the night blurred by in a daze of dancing, speeches, and small tea plates of food. Annaleigh briefly registered her mother coming up to her, kissing her with tears in her eyes, and her father following close behind. As gracefully as possible,

Annaleigh made her way around the rooms, thanking everyone for spending the night with them as their guest. Mary urged them on, shepherding her and William around in an attempt to keep them busy until exhaustion threatened to drag them to the ground, under the clomping feet of the dancers.

The night deepened, and the crowd seemed to grow denser and louder as the drinks flowed more freely. The music came faster. The large skirts became more awkward and clumsy to move about. The comfortable crowdedness of the parlor began to overwhelm Annaleigh, though no one took much notice. Her cheeks flushed with heat and her head grew fuzzy. The corset pinched uncomfortably at her ribs and her breath was coming too quick and too shallow. Before she fainted in the middle of the dance floor, she pulled William close to her and whispered in his ear.

"I need some air."

"Anything for you," he said, taking her hand to lead her out the front door.

As they crossed through the foyer, a large, round man with a bushy, gray beard clapped William across the back and bellowed a great laugh.

"I was wondering when I'd have a chance to congratulate you, boy. Our town has been waiting for this wedding for quite some time now. I remember when the two of you were younger, how you'd run through the market, and that one time... The box of peaches—" He bent over to laugh, sloshing his drink to the ground. "Old Jefferson hadn't even seen you comin', and suddenly there he was, knocked to his ass and covered in preserves!"

Annaleigh shifted from foot to foot, squeezing William's hand. One look at her panicked eyes told him that she couldn't stay inside for much longer. She needed the cool, brisk air of open space. She wanted wind and ice and room to breathe.

"How could I forget?" William said with a smile.

As the man launched into another half-story muddled by his drunkenness, William leaned into Annaleigh.

"Go. I'll meet you down by the lake. Ten minutes," he said.

"Make it five."

"Done." He kissed her gently, taking his hand from hers to trace the soft curve of her neck down to her shoulders. "You look beautiful."

She stepped away and smiled teasingly. "So do you."

As she hurried down the front steps and followed the twisting pathway to the river, she looked back at the house. William was framed in the bright doorway, always the perfect host, playing along with every story and laughing at the appropriate times. He was being especially patient tonight; it must be his way of placating Mary. When he laughed, he threw his head back. He caught her watching him out of the corner of his eye and his smile deepened to something more sincere.

He held up his hand, mouthing, "Three minutes."

A woman in a simple dress walked up behind William and placed a hand on his shoulder. She was tall and lithe, with dark hair piled in an old-fashioned way. Something about the way she looked tickled the back of Annaleigh's mind. William didn't turn at the woman's touch, but Mary appeared right away, saying something to draw the woman away from him. The way Mary glanced frantically around the room almost made Annaleigh turn around and return to the reception. Was she looking for her? She should at least tell her that she needed to step away for a moment to get some air…

But just the idea of going back into the wall of heat made her face flush, so she turned around and hurried away from the house, out of view of the prying guests.

The moon followed her down to the lake, which appeared black and bottomless. The woods were quiet and the shore was empty except for the chairs that had been left from the ceremony. The bony-white backs of the seats reminded her of skeletons silently watching. It was eerily beautiful, both breathtaking and haunting.

She walked down the aisle of skeletons to the archway she had stood under just hours ago. If she closed her eyes, she could relive every single moment of the ceremony. She could imagine William standing next to her in his brilliant suit, Mary with her flowers.

Mary had been right for planning every small detail of the wedding. At the time, Annaleigh had thought she was going overboard, but it had been worth it. Every tiny question had led to a miraculous scene of beauty. The wedding, the reception— Mary had worked magic. Annaleigh would have to remember to thank her tonight, after everyone left.

Lifting the heavy, white skirts of her wedding dress, she stepped away from the arch and onto the rickety dock that stretched out over the lake. She wanted to be closer to the water, to dip her fingers in and see if it had warmed from the short burst of spring heat they had gotten earlier in the week or if it still held the ice of winter. The heels of her shoes wobbled on the uneven planks, and she made a mental note to see that the dock is rebuilt for the summer. When was the last time someone had replaced the wood?

The end of the dock stopped just before the deepest part of the lake, where the sandy shelf of the shore dropped off into the dark depths. When she and William were younger, they had tried to see how far the floor of the lake dropped, but they never had enough breath for their toes to even brush the bottom. She doubted they had even gotten close.

She set her skirts down, not bothering to pull the edges up when they skimmed the surface of the lake. Mary would throw a fit, but the water looked clean enough, and she'd never wear the dress again. Annaleigh didn't see the harm in it now.

Carefully, she knelt down, reaching her hand to the water. The moon cut out her silhouette on the dark lake. The water bit her fingers coldly. It took only a moment for her to lose feeling in her fingertips, but then the water began to feel warm. A curl fell down into her face, and she didn't bother pushing it back before she dipped her other hand into the lake.

A noise—as soft as a whisper—came from behind Annaleigh. She quickly pulled her hands from the water, expecting to find William standing there, shaking his head at her. She scanned the shore and found no one. For the briefest moment, she thought she had seen someone seated in one of the skeleton chairs, but she blinked and they were gone.

Exhaustion, her mind excused itself.

Annaleigh gathered up her skirts to stand, her heels teetering on the boards of the dock. She took a few uneven steps backward before she set down the bottom of her heavy dress. Again, she scanned the shore, searching for William. She looked up to the house but couldn't make out any figures there either.

When she spun around, a shadow blocked her view of the abandoned chairs. A loud caw tore through the silence of the night as a raven with feathers that glistened midnight swooped right in front of her. It dove toward her, attempting to snatch the gleaming locket at her throat. The bird missed but circled back to try again. Annaleigh swatted at it, stumbling back, closer to the water.

The raven's screech sent a shudder through her bones, and when it swooped once more, it force Annaleigh to take another shaky step back, out of its way. Suddenly, she was tripping over the hem of her wedding dress, falling as the bird flew off into the dark woods.

Annaleigh twisted awkwardly and crashed hard, toppling onto the wet boards of the dock. Her breath was knocked from her lungs, and the silence that returned to the lake was broken by a skittering metal sound and a soft *plunk*.

Before she even caught her breath again, she rolled onto her stomach, giving up any hope at keeping her wedding dress clean. She pulled herself to the edge of the dock and looked over.

The necklace sank slowly in the moonlit water, its chain following the heavy locket, like a ribbon fluttering in the breeze.

"No!"

She crawled to her knees and dove her hand into the water, her fingers groping uselessly at the locket already out of reach. She leaned forward more, stretching her arm as far as she could. The water turned her numb and made her reflexes too slow, her fingers barely missing the chain.

A breeze pulled more curls from her hair and pushed them into her face, obscuring her vision. Behind her, she thought she could hear a voice on the wind, but her focus was on the lake and the locket. She couldn't lose it…

She gritted her teeth in determination, dug her fingers into the soggy boards of the dock to hold herself steady, and leaned even closer to the water, making one last grab at the locket.

Her fingers hooked around the top of the chain in the nick of time, saving it from the seemingly bottomless lake. She held it up in triumph, the locket swinging above the rotting dock, but she had miscalculated her balance. Too much of her dress had fallen into the water in front of her, weighing her down as the fabric soaked through with the freezing water of the lake. She had leaned over too far. Her weight shifted forward and she toppled over into the black lake, breaking the smooth surface and abandoning the locket on the dock.

Surprised by the sudden shock of icy water, she opened her mouth. The arctic water raced to her lungs and pain laced through her entire body. Alarm pulsed insistently in her head, her thoughts screaming as her lungs begged for air. With a bulk of her skirts clutched in one hand, she tried to swim up while she could still tell where up was. She broke the surface of the lake for a moment and meant to scream for help but only ended up coughing and gulping down more water.

Her wedding dress grew even heavier still, continuing to weigh her down. It pulled Annaleigh deeper and deeper into the darkest part of the lake. She felt like she was *burning*, like her veins had caught fire and seared in her head and lungs. How could she be burning in water?

Invisible fingers constricted around her throat, and she did her best not to gasp from the cold that stiffened her muscles and made her feel sluggish. Everything was happening too quickly, and she was moving so painfully slow.

Air. I need to breathe!

The wedding dress twisted around her, tangling around her legs like the inverted petals of a flower closing in the cold. Annaleigh fought hard against the pull of her waterlogged skirts, did her best to try to tear away some of the fabric that was sinking her faster than she'd thought possible. But the fabric held true—she couldn't even pop one stitch—so she abandoned that effort in exchange for battling her way back to the surface. She wouldn't give in to the small part of her brain that said she should just close her eyes and sleep. That it would be so easy to fall...

No. She could swim—she was a *good* swimmer—and she would not drown. The lake would not get the satisfaction of becoming her coffin. Legs thrashing, arms pulling, muscles screaming, she struggled to stay afloat near the surface. If she drifted too far, there would be no hope—

In the freezing water, dragged down by the unbearable weight of her wedding dress, her strength sapped quickly.

Through stinging eyes, she could only murkily see the slow-motion dance of her hair and skirts. In her foggy mind, she found it beautiful to be so impossibly weightless. It was a feeling that was at odds with the heaviness she held inside herself.

One slow blink disoriented her entirely. She couldn't tell which way was up, but she somehow knew she was falling.

The pain in her chest and head became too much, and she let out a scream that was silenced by the water around her that rushed back into her lungs to fill her to brimming. It was too much. Annaleigh couldn't remember why she was holding her breath, so she breathed in lungful after lungful of water, confused as to why it brought her no relief.

Sinking felt like a dream. Engulfed by blackness, Annaleigh floated through a starless space. Her chest screamed for air, for anything other than water, but she was too tired to listen anymore. As she closed her eyes, she swore she could still feel the weight of the locket in her hand, the feeling of the chain knotted around her cold fingers.

In the sluggish hallucinations of her mind, she thought she saw the face of William's mother behind her eyelids—beautiful Sara, who looked so much like her son did when he was concerned, eyebrows pinched and lips pressed. She had the strangest eyes, a molten golden that was flecked with sparks of calm gray. Annaleigh recognized those eyes…

Distantly, she wondered if she was dying, if she would finally get to meet William's mother. Annaleigh had always wondered what they'd talk about.

Sara reached out a gentle hand. Her whisper silenced the last of the fear in Annaleigh's mind.

Rest, sweet girl.

The voice was so familiar. Like a song long forgotten…

When Annaleigh finally passed out, there was no relief. She couldn't tell the difference between drowning and oblivion, but her head grew foggy and rational thought escaped her in those final moments. *It's not all that bad.*

Her feet skimmed the bottom of the lake just as the surface cracked open in a sudden surge of waves and bubbles. Suddenly, she remembered which way was up. It did her no good.

CHAPTER 11

The Plea

SHE WAS HEAVIER THAN HE'D expected, and William nearly went down with her. But he had a surprising strength in the wintry water, and when he saw her drifting down into the darkest parts of the lake he'd never be able to reach, he knew if he lost her, he would lose himself. Either they both surfaced or neither of them would.

Haloed by hair and shrouded in the eddying lace of her wedding dress, she looked like an angel asleep. Her head lulled back and her mouth opened, and he saw the last of her breath escape in a stream of small, slow bubbles. William steadied his hold around her center, fighting her cumbersome dress as he pulled them both back to the surface. The lake would not have the privilege of keeping her tonight. She was his and he was hers.

The locket pulled at his neck as he fought the pull of the lake, a noose of a warning. He had seen the moonlight sparkle off its gold face when he was halfway down the hillside. That's when he knew something was wrong. She never took it off, not once since he'd proposed to her. He sprinted the rest of the distance to the lake, scooped up the locket, and called for her. Silence screamed back at him. She was nowhere.

Then the black water rippled beneath him, a gasp of bubbles floated across its face, and he barely had enough sense to kick off his shoes and throw down his jacket before he jumped in the lake, too.

By the time he surfaced with Annaleigh, her lips were blue. He sucked in air greedily, but his heart sank back into the water when he felt how still she was in his arms.

With all of the strength he had left, he swam to shore. The cold had caught up to him by the time he was in the shallows of the lake, and his knees sank into the gritty sand as he crawled out of the water with her, shaking with a violent chill.

As gently as he could, he laid Annaleigh down in front of him. His head was pounding from the cold and all of his muscles howled for him to just lie down next to her and sleep forever, but he couldn't let her go. He slid his fingers to her wrist, checking for a pulse, but he found nothing. The locket swung from his neck and settled on her chest as he moved his hand to her face, his head to her heart—wishing harder than he ever had before.

"I ask for nothing," he whispered harshly to the universe. "Nothing but her."

He let his fingers find the paleness of her neck, his lips find the clamminess of her temple, and he closed his eyes as he bargained with whatever angels or devils were listening.

If anyone had been watching, they would have thought that William and Annaleigh were nothing but shadows on the shore, two mysterious lovers shrouded by the night. It wasn't until a sob broke the back of William that it was clear the moment wasn't one of tenderness, but rather one that shattered his perception of the universe. In the silence of her heart, he lost everything good he had found in the world.

Hopelessness was a black hole that destroyed everything. William's life slipped out of its orbit, and he was spinning, lost, without a tether. Without a *purpose*.

And then, against all reason, she opened her eyes, and his world repaired itself all at once. He came back down from the heavens of stars and was grounded next to her, but he couldn't convince his lungs that it was safe to breathe again, even as she rolled over and coughed up two lungfuls of lake water.

"*Annaleigh*." It was a word sighed in relief and grief, barely brighter than the moonlight.

The air didn't feel right to Annaleigh. As she breathed it in, she found herself wishing for the water again. It had been peaceful there, once the panic had subsided. If only she could…

A sense of wrong prickled at her back and sent a chill up her spine. She shuddered in her sopping-wet, sand-covered wedding dress and felt the hot press of hysteria at the backs of her eyes.

"You're alive. I'm here."

William ran his hands up her arm, trying to steal the winter that had turned to ice inside her, but Annaleigh jerked away from him, scared, in pain. He nearly reached for her again, but he let his hands flutter just above her, searching for a way to help.

She rolled over and found William. He looked like a disaster, half broken with misery and tentatively strengthened by hope. In a distant corner of Annaleigh's mind, she wondered what had happened to his jacket. At least Mary wouldn't be mad that *everything* they were wearing was ruined. He was only in his white undershirt, and his sleeves were pushed up to his elbows. The wet shirt and pants clung to him, constricting him in a cold embrace. His dark hair dripped down his face and his concerned gray eyes—no longer glinting with playfulness—took every bit of her in wondrously.

He studied her like a blind man who had been gifted temporary sight, as if this were the first time he was seeing her and he'd never get another chance to behold her again. He had to make *this moment* count before it was too late.

"William—" She choked on his name, her voice scraped raw by the word.

He set his hands on her, trying to hold her together before she shattered apart from coughing, but he felt her twitch under his hands as if he were causing her pain. He pulled back, but only slightly.

How amazing, William thought, how thin the line between life and death was. It was stretched and pulled thin across a person, tying them up so delicately that one wrong move could snap the tenuous thread of life. Annaleigh had come too close— *he* had come too close.

"I thought…" Even without water in his lungs, he found it hard to breathe, nearly impossible to speak. "I thought I'd lost you."

Annaleigh reached up a hand to place on his heart, wincing. Her touch was light and cold, so cold he could feel it even through his sopping shirt.

"You're absolutely freezing, Anna." He slid his fingers over her cheeks again, and his hand felt like fire to her. He burned so hot that it was painful to have him touch her, but she didn't want him to stop, so she said nothing. "Anna," he whispered again, lost in thought as he searched the woods and the hillside then looked back over the lake. She was confused as to why he wasn't saying her full name, but he was too shaken to notice his slip. "My jacket… Let me get you my jacket. You're frozen through."

He stood as if to leave, to return to the dock where he had left his shoes and jacket, but she grabbed his fingers and pulled him back down to her.

"Stay," was all she could manage.

He sank back down to his knees. With shaking fingers, he traced every inch of her he could reach as the moon lingered high in the sky. She was ice cold and a startling pale that made her skin so translucent that it appeared nearly blue, almost the exact same blue as her dress on New Year's.

Even though she felt like winter in his arms, she never shivered once. Just before he began to worry about what that meant, Annaleigh regained her voice.

"Mary is going to hate me." She cleared her throat again, finding more words. "I ruined my dress. Completely destroyed it."

Relief cracked his chest open, and he laughed. The laugh sounded wounded, edging near hysteria. "Mary will be glad you're *alive*."

Another finger of disbelief trailed up Annaleigh's spine and sent a shiver of goose bumps across her body.

"Are you cold?" William asked, taking her hands between his.

"No," she said, shaking her head, confused.

She wasn't cold at all, but she felt strange... Out of place, distant. Like the world was too much with her in it.

Everything was loud and bright and uncomfortable. It was probably shock, she told herself. Surely, after nearly drowning, she would feel strange. But she hadn't expected to feel a sense of loss. She brought her hands up to her neck, thinking about how close she had come to never breathing again. She went to twine the chain of the locket around her fingers but realized it was missing.

"The locket!"

"It's here. I have it," William said, removing the locket from himself. "I saw it on the dock. You never take it off, and I knew... What happened?"

She watched the locket swing from his fingers, hardly registering his words. He reached out to put the locket on her again, but she stayed his hands.

"Will you keep it? Please?"

There was something about the necklace that made her uneasy now. Maybe it was how close she had come to losing it forever in the depths of the lake. Having an heirloom with such significance behind it made her anxious. If anything happened to it, she could never forgive herself.

William watched her, studying her face worriedly. He was transfixed by her eyes, which seemed so shockingly bright in the moonlight. There was an impossible lightness to them, a blue that had no right to exist in such a dull world. He didn't realize how unnatural they looked next to the waxy pallor of her skin; he didn't seem to notice her stillness.

"Of course I will," he said, putting the locket in his pocket.

"Just for now," Annaleigh explained. "I nearly lost it once already. Just…please, hold on to it until I'm ready to take it back?"

"Whatever you wish," he said, taking her hand again. "Can you stand?"

It took an absurd amount of time for her to find her legs and make them cooperate enough for her to stand up. Even with William's help, she felt insubstantial. Something wasn't right.

"Annaleigh?"

"I'm just feeling…a little…lightheaded," she said, hands clawing at the back of her corset. The dress was too tight, too heavy with water, and she was still much too weak to bear it.

"Are you sure you can—" William's voice sounded deep and very far away as blackness filled Annaleigh's vision and she fell back to the shore. In fainting, she returned to the water.

She felt the world rocking her to sleep.

She felt the caress of fabric slipping over her.

She felt pressure on her arms and legs and then lightness all over.

She felt the burn of lips touching to her forehead.

She felt surrounded then alone and on fire.

And then she heard a voice. It was a sobbing sound, muffled nearly to silence by something—a hand or a handkerchief. But who was crying underwater?

Slowly, as if her eyelashes were made of iron that weighed her lids low into sleep, she opened her eyes. She was back in her bedroom, lying on her bed in a light nightgown with a hot washcloth on her forehead. It was too hot—so hot she could feel her skin searing below it. With a hiss, she threw it off of her and it landed with a dull, wet thud on the ground.

The sob stopped short, as if swallowed.

Annaleigh kicked at the heavy blankets that were laid over her. She felt trapped under them, and she didn't want them to touch her anymore. She didn't want anyone or anything to touch her. Feverishly, she fought off the blankets and tripped out of her bed, stumbling into the dresser.

The mirror shook above her, rocking back and forth. When she caught her strange, pale reflection, she nearly screamed. She fell back, away from the dresser, her reflection, the bed, and the cascade of blankets that littered the ground. She pushed herself back until she was standing in the far corner of her bedroom, far away from everything around her that seemed too big and *not right*.

Feeling panicked and cornered, she looked around her room. Her skin was crawling; her head was spinning. She was freezing but burning hot, and she could swear that, if she moved too suddenly, she could still feel water sloshing in her lungs.

"Anna?" Another sob tore at the silence and her nerves.

Her gaze jumped to the sound. *Mary.*

"Anna?" Mary lifted both of her hands in a sign of surrender. She moved slowly away from the door and closer to her corner. "Please, I'm not going to hurt you. I know you're scared, all right? Just—please don't scream. Don't bring Will in here."

Of course she's not going to hurt me, Annaleigh thought, but for some reason, she pressed herself farther into the corner.

Mary moved until she was just an arm's length away from Annaleigh. Her face was red and streaked with tears, her eyes clean of makeup but rimmed with pink. How long had she been crying?

"No one knows what happened… Everyone went home already. It's only us," she said, keeping her hands raised, palms out. "It's just me."

The muscles in Annaleigh's arms and legs relaxed a little, as if whatever threat they'd perceived had evaporated.

"I'm going to touch you now, okay? It's going to feel strange, but I just… I have to hug you, Anna."

Annaleigh was about to ask what would feel strange when Mary closed the space between them and hugged her with more tenderness than she ever had before. It wasn't Mary's typical hug, excited and rough. It was careful; it was painfully hot.

She could feel Mary's small body shaking against her, but she could do nothing to stop it. She couldn't even find her voice to say anything to help. Annaleigh could only stand there in the corner, her arms by her sides and her hands clenched in fists against the burning pain.

"Mary?" Her voice sounded like crystal dropped to the ground, shattering into a thousand pieces. "What's happening to me?"

In another broken sob, Mary's words breezed over Annaleigh's ear. *"He was too late."*

Part 3

And this was the reason that, long ago,
In this kingdom by the sea,
A wind blew out of a cloud, chilling
My beautiful Annabel Lee;
So that her highborn kinsmen came
And bore her away from me,
To shut her up in a sepulchre
In this kingdom by the sea.

— Stanza III, *Annabel Lee* by Edgar Allan Poe

CHAPTER 12

A Burn

MARY'S WORDS BUZZED IN THE air like angry bees, and Annaleigh's head began to pound in earnest, a headache forming a knot at the top of her spine and wringing her of her sanity. The things Mary was saying weren't making sense—nothing was making sense. The world was on fire and Annaleigh was the only one in the universe aware of the heat. She was the only one wrapped in its blaze.

Annaleigh felt like her skin was peeling itself back, rolling away to expose muscle and tendon and blood, and she just wanted to live in the oblivion of unconsciousness again. It was easier there. That pain seemed like nothing compared to this.

She shook against Mary as she opened her mouth and tried to speak again. "It...*hurts*..."

Mary leaned back from Annaleigh, carefully removing her hands. "What hurts? What hurts, Anna? What can I do?" Without touching her, she looked her over for the source of pain but found nothing.

"*Hurts*," Annaleigh said again, her voice sounding foreign with agony.

"I don't see—" Mary turned away from Annaleigh. "Mother, please help. I can't do anything to help her. I don't know what to do… Oh *God,* what do I do?"

Annaleigh's vision blurred as the room tilted, streaks of light shooting across her eyes. Her head throbbed so severely that she was sure she'd be sick. She couldn't make sense of what Mary was saying; she couldn't even properly hear her through the shrieks of agony inside her own mind. But she did catch one word and it was enough to make her hang on to her consciousness a little longer: *mother.*

"Please," Mary begged the darkness behind her.

Unable to support herself on her shaky legs anymore, Annaleigh slid down the wall. She landed hard on the floor, knees pulled up to her chest. Every point of contact—the wall, the floor, her nightgown—threatened to set her ablaze.

She wanted to be surrounded by nothingness again, but the world wasn't that kind. She tried looking up at Mary again and thought she saw someone standing in front of her. It was the woman from the party, the one who'd laid her hand on William's shoulder and had been quickly whisked away by Mary.

The woman was slightly taller than Mary but in every other way appeared her mirror. She was slender, with hair so dark it seemed like the universe had torn open around her shoulders. Her eyes were the same warm amber of Mary's, bright and golden but with stormy slices of silver. The same silver as William's.

The warmth the woman carried inside her raked Annaleigh's body with chills so violently painful that she doubled forward onto her knees. This was Sara.

Annaleigh recognized her now that she wasn't wearing the raspberry mask she'd first seen her in. Sara was the woman who had spoken to her on New Year's, the one she'd seen in the crowd at her wedding, the woman waiting by William's shoulder that fateful night.

"Mary..." Annaleigh's voice was barely a whimper, and only Sara seemed to hear.

"Please," Mary continued, begging her mother. "I can't help her!" She shook her head. "I can't do anything... I can't tell him. He wouldn't believe me. He wouldn't... He wouldn't *survive* this. You saw what happened with father, after you. Will is worse than that. Worse! She's all he has. You have to do something. Help me—help *her*."

"I can do nothing, Mary." Sara's voice was deep and beautiful, and it was torture for Annaleigh. She'd always imagined what she sounded like when Mary used to regale her with stories of how lovely she sang. But nothing she'd imagined had ever come close to this.

"I reject that out of hand!" Mary said, her own voice rising. "You can do something. You have to. You saved Will before, and you can save her now."

"I did not save your brother," Sara said with sadness in her eyes as she looked at Mary and then past her, studying Annaleigh. Annaleigh shrank into herself further, a daisy hiding from a storm. "She did."

"You sent her to the house that day! You said... You said if she hadn't shown up when she did, if she had left when Samuel said he wasn't having visitors, he would have hanged himself."

"But I did not intervene. Fate did. I have explained this to you, Mary." She reached for her daughter and took her hand. "I cannot change what is to be. I cannot change what has become. It's too late."

Mary shook her head over and over, so fast that all of her curls fell around her shoulders. "No. *NO!*"

"Keep your voice down, Mary," Sara said, looking over her shoulder to the door. "William is just down the hall."

Annaleigh felt sick. "I'm hallucinating," she said to herself, out loud, as if hearing the words would be enough to convince herself. Because none of this made even the smallest bit of sense. But madness—*that* made more sense than everything she was seeing, everything she was hearing and feeling. "I'm dreaming."

"What curse have I been given, then?" Mary asked, collapsing onto the bed, looking even paler than Annaleigh on the floor. "That I can *see* what will happen but do nothing to stop it? That I can *see* her now, knowing she's gone forever? That I've lost both a mother and a sister?"

The tears were falling down Mary's cheeks, smearing what was left of her makeup and washing her face entirely bare.

"I did everything I could, moving their wedding," she continued. "The trees and flowers by the river had not even bloomed yet. I saw her drowning with flowers. When it was *warmer*. She died in the light of morning, not midnight. I would not have had them married yesterday if I had known my visions were bloody lies!" She cursed in French.

"You saw only what you could bear, Mary," Sara said.

Annaleigh moaned from the floor, covering her ears from the loudness of the room. It was all too much. The world rocked beneath her knees, and she could swear she was sitting in a very small boat in a riotous sea. But when she clawed her fingers into the floor, she could feel the lacquered wood of her bedroom, the fraying edge of the rug under her bed.

"I saw her *drown*. How could I bear that?"

Annaleigh felt the world tilt, could swear it started spinning the wrong way. *Drowned?*

"Shh, Mary." Sara stepped closer to Mary and sat down next to her on the bed. She made no noise, and none of the blankets shifted under her. "You needed to prepare yourself for what would happen, but if you knew when…"

"I wouldn't have let her out of my sight," Mary said fiercely. "I would've told fate to pucker up and lay its stupid lips on my—"

"*Mary.*"

Mary bowed her head, her fists loosening as the fight drained from her. "I've seen her die twice now. How can I tell Will? How can he even *see* her? How is it possible?"

"The locket. You know the power it holds. Don't let him take it off. As for what you tell him, you say nothing, yet. What happens next decides many things. One wrong step—"

"And I lose Will, too," Mary finished. "I'm going to be sick." Her skirts hissed as she jumped to her feet and ran out of the room, closing the door as quietly as she could behind her, leaving Sara and Annaleigh alone.

The candles lit next to the bed fizzled out in a swirl of smoke. The room was doused with darkness, giving Annaleigh's eyes a merciful reprieve. Surprisingly, she found that she had no problem seeing in the veil of night that shrouded her bedroom. In fact, she could see better without the bleary streaks of light in her eyes. Her skin still felt as if it were being boiled off, a pain that ate away at her bones, but it was easier in the dark. She opened her eyes again, watched as Sara soundlessly made her way over and kneeled in front of her.

"Annaleigh," Sara said quietly, carefully. She smiled, but it was a heartbreaking smile that was ragged and torn with sadness. "I've been waiting for so long to meet you. I had rather hoped… I didn't expect it to be quite so soon."

"*How?*" was all Annaleigh could manage.

Sara's smile fell. She looked so strikingly like Mary, and it was hard for Annaleigh to remember who she was speaking to. It was easier for her to accept that Mary had grown older through the night than to believe she was talking to Sara. To Sara, who had been dead for years.

I've gone mad.

"Everything must be so confusing," Sara said. "I remember when I first… It was horrible. Overwhelming."

Annaleigh nodded, numb.

"It gets easier. Parts of it, at least. The pain subsides once you come to accept it. It's like fear, in a way. When you acknowledge it and succumb, you come to control it instead of letting it control you."

"I fell," Annaleigh said haltingly. "The lake. Your locket. It fell. I didn't mean to be so clumsy with it."

"Oh, sweet girl." Sara reached out a hand to rest on her cheek.

Annaleigh cowered away, expecting the pain of another touch, but when she felt cool fingers gently pushing back her hair from her face, there was no pain. No burning agony. It was as soft as the caress of the wind.

"You have nothing to apologize for," Sarah said. "*I'm* sorry."

"My head hurts." It was easier for Annaleigh to speak now. She wasn't sure if it was the dark or the fact that, for the first time since she'd surfaced from the lake, a touch hadn't hurt her, but the words were easier to find. "I feel…dizzy. I don't know how I can see you. How *Mary* can see you…"

Sara folded her hands in her lap and listened.

"I ruined my wedding dress," Annaleigh said suddenly, remembering. "Was Mary mad?"

"Not about the dress."

"Oh, good. I was worried." She found her legs under her and stood, feeling much better than before. "I have to go find William now. I feel like I should be with him."

"Not yet, dear." Sara reached up and took her hand, guiding her back to the floor.

"I thought I saw you at our wedding," Annaleigh admitted. "I thought I was losing my mind."

"I was there. You looked radiant, and William was so happy. Happier than I've ever seen him. He had a look to him that made me think he'd swindled Heaven of its finest angel. I think he did." Sara took Annaleigh's hand and turned it over in her own. She traced the intricate setting of her engagement ring and wedding band. "Thank you for loving him, for reminding him what was worth living for. I am *so sorry*."

Why does she keep apologizing? Annaleigh thought, but she shrugged it off. If this was a dream—or if it wasn't—she had so many things she wanted to ask Sara. "So Mary can see you?"

"Mary…" Sara pursed her lips, thinking. "She can see many things. I am only one of them."

"And here I thought she couldn't keep a secret to save her life." Annaleigh shook her head. "And you've always been here?"

"Mostly."

Annaleigh let out a small laugh. "Then the rumors about the Calloway house being haunted were correct. How funny."

Sara nodded. "Tell me what happened, Annaleigh."

"When?"

"At the lake."

Another chill shook Annaleigh's bones, and fogginess muddled her mind. She didn't feel like talking about the lake. "I should find William."

"You said you almost lost my locket?"

"William has it now. I can go and get it from him." Annaleigh nearly stood again, but Sara's hand stilled her.

There were voices coming from the hallway. It sounded like William was talking with Mary about something. Or arguing. It sounded more like arguing. She wished she could hear them better, wished Sara would let her leave the room.

"The lake?" Sara asked again.

Annaleigh wished Sara would stop asking about the lake. "It was cold," she finally answered. "The locket had fallen off, and it landed in the water. When I went to reach for it, I fell."

Sara nodded, encouraging her to go on.

"I saved the locket." Her memories were blurry, like her vision when she'd opened her eyes under water. "And then my dress... it was so heavy. If he weren't such a great swimmer, William never would have been able to save me. If *I* weren't such a good swimmer, he never would have even had the chance."

"My William saved you?" Sara asked, a strange look in her eyes. She watched Annaleigh as if her answer would tell her something very important.

"He's incredibly strong."

"He saved you?" she asked again.

"Of course. I told him to hold on to the locket until I didn't feel so clumsy. I know how much it means to him and Mary. He pretends he isn't still affected by the memory of you, but I know he is," Annaleigh said. "I should get William. He would love to see you again, if only for a moment—"

"No, Annaleigh." Sara stood, her skirts swirling around her legs without shifting any air in front of Annaleigh. "He can't see me. Not now."

"Please. Just let me go to him. I need to see William." She stood with Sara. "I think he's just outside."

"Annaleigh, listen to me," Sara said, putting her hands on her shoulders.

"I'm feeling much better," Annaleigh insisted. "I need to see William."

"Annaleigh... William—he was too late."

Too late, for what?

"No, he's just outside the door," she said, shaking her head. Her hair was loose and wild, gold knots hanging around her shoulders. "Let me get him. He'll tell you."

"Annaleigh, you didn't come back from the lake," Sara said.

Of course I did. I'm here. Mary's here...

Sara kept speaking as Annaleigh's mind argued back, screaming how *wrong wrong wrong* everything she was saying was.

"He was too late. Your dress was too heavy. Do you remember that? It pulled you down to the very bottom of the lake. You both were never able to find the bottom, remember? It was always too deep."

"How do you know that?" *Why does she keep asking if I remember? This is a horrible dream,* Annaleigh decided. "I want to wake up now."

"You are awake, Annaleigh. I'm sorry."

"Stop apologizing," Annaleigh said, terror creeping up her throat.

"It's all I have to offer you. I'm sorry this happened to you, and I'm so, so sorry I have to tell you like this. But William will be in here soon. Mary can't hold him long..."

The voices behind the door rose. "She needs her rest, Will!"

"There's not enough time for me to tell you how important this is," Sara continued, rushing her words. "He cannot know yet, Annaleigh. It would end him. You didn't survive."

"Yes, I did," Annaleigh insisted. But the more Sara pushed, the more unreal everything felt. Her reality felt like a falsehood, and her resolve was starting to unravel.

"I was there, next to you, when you drowned. You saw me. I was there to greet you when your heart stopped."

"No..." Now Annaleigh felt like Mary, shaking her head and sitting too quickly on the bed.

"Your dress was heavy, you sank too deep, and your lungs filled with water as you..."

Screamed. The pain returned to Annaleigh. The sensation of her lungs ripping apart, waiting for air. The heavy confusion of swallowing so much water that she could swear her vision had turned blue. The rocks at the bottom of the lake beneath her feet…

"But William—"

"Saved part of you. But not *you*."

"What does that mean? What does that make me?" Panic rose and fell rapidly inside Annaleigh's throat, reason and logic fighting her memories. Memories she *knew* were real—too vivid and painful to be made up. She'd died, but she was here. She was gone, yet remained. She was *dead*…

"Am I a ghost?" Annaleigh's head surged with sickness again. Her skin was hot, and she felt the sensation she'd had on the beach again. The *wrongness*, the *insubstantiality* of it all.

"Mary calls us specters. Echoes of our life, energy trapped somewhere between this world and whatever is next."

"Whatever is next?"

"For the dead…" Sara completed carefully. "For those like us."

"Why?" Her voice rose, and Sara cautioned her with a look to the door. "Why am I still here? Why do I have to be here if I'm dead?"

"Oh, Annaleigh." Sara stepped closer to touch her again, but Annaleigh backed away, wary. Her arm was half extended to Annaleigh, awkwardly hanging in the air. She lowered it, disappointed, apologetic. "Sweet girl. You're not done yet."

"Done with what?"

Just then, the door slammed open and Mary was trying to block William from coming inside, her arms and legs spread wide to take up the space in the doorframe. Sara disappeared and Annaleigh was left staring at the empty space between her and the bed.

"Mary, for God's sake, get out of my way. I want to see my wife!" William pushed his way past Mary, and she spun around, eyes wide with panic.

"She's not rested, William. The cold, um… She's very tired, hallucinating a little. Still sore…"

Annaleigh looked back at Mary, matching her uneasiness.

"Look, she's fine," William said, gesturing to Annaleigh. "She's up already. Not even resting!"

"She's *supposed* to be." Mary shook her head at Annaleigh behind his back.

Annaleigh managed to put on a smile though she was sure it was thoroughly unconvincing. "It's all right, Mary." *No it isn't.*

"See, Mary? It's all right." William turned back to her and nodded his head to the door. "We're fine. No chaperones needed. Please leave me with my wife."

"I really should—"

"No, Mary, you shouldn't." He escorted her to the door. "See you in the morning."

Annaleigh caught the terrified look of Mary, Sara standing over her shoulder, just before William closed the door.

"There," he said, turning the lock to ensure that Mary wouldn't intrude on them again. "Much better."

As he turned to face Annaleigh again, he lit one of the candles on the nightstand. Pain shot behind Annaleigh's eyes again, but she tried to hide it from him. She fixed her features into a mask of calm, which splintered apart when he touched her.

His hands on her here, his fingers tracing nonsense across her skin now, was excruciatingly more painful than it had been at the lake. Annaleigh felt like she had been exposed and raw for too long. Even the slightest brush or caress felt like hell, but she bore it all in silence.

How would she survive this?

Before he caught the anguish that was wringing her dry, stealing away all of her composure, she fell into his chest, hugging him and hiding her face from him.

She burned all over, but she would accept the pain if it saved him his.

"My wife," he repeated. "My Annaleigh." He ran his hand through her hair, down her back. "Mary was right... You do need to rest. But there's no reason I can't rest with you."

"The locket... You still have it?"

He stepped back from her and pulled the long chain of the locket from his pocket. "Safe and sound."

"Don't take it off," she told him.

He gave her a strange look but nodded.

As he led her to bed, helped her under the covers, and slid in next to her, she couldn't help but think of the dark embrace of the lake. Her skin screamed when he put his arm around her and kissed her goodnight. She clamped her jaw closed so the screams couldn't escape their prison within her.

"I'm never letting you go again," he whispered to her. "I will never come that close to losing you ever again in all of my life. I swear I will keep you safe. My wife."

"I love you, William."

He murmured his love into the hollow of her throat. He didn't notice the stillness, the missing pulse he had once kept time with, marking the tempo with his lips.

She felt him fall asleep behind her, but she lay rigidly awake through the entire night, remembering.

She'd never surfaced from the lake. Her body was still down there, tangled in her wedding dress. Was her skin blue? Were her eyes open? Would anyone ever find her?

For the briefest moment, Sara appeared before her. She placed her hand over William's on Annaleigh's arm and frowned. "I'm so sorry, my son...my daughter," she said, looking to Annaleigh. "You both deserved so much more." She disappeared, taking the light from the candle with her.

"*It hurts*," Annaleigh whispered back, but she didn't just mean the searing pain of contact.

Her chest ached, more so than it had when she was drowning. It was a different kind of suffocation, an overwhelming ache that came from within. Her heart was constricted in a sadness she had never known.

Just hours ago, she had married. When their lips had touched, it had tasted of forever. Now, in the darkness of her bedroom, she thought about everything they would never have. Their forever had lasted mere hours.

Years of their life together, not yet spent and gone, flashed behind her eyes. The dances they should have shared, the places they would have visited… The child she would have had — a son with her pale hair and his dangerous eyes, or a daughter with William's brilliant cheeks and her stubborn mouth. What a spectacular aunt Mary would have made. What a perfect family they would have made.

As her heart split apart, she let silent tears fall on her pillow.

It was too late for that life. It had gone before she'd even had a chance to begin living it. Alone with William, she was trapped in the tomb of her own mind, mourning the future they should have enjoyed together but never would. In the deepest hours of the night, she thought that the pain of death itself was nothing. It was the bookends of drowning that had ruined her — the immediate agony of before and the everything after.

CHAPTER 13

A Vision

MORNING CAME TOO SOON, BRINGING with it the searing pain of inescapable daylight. It was odd for Annaleigh to go on through the day pretending that nothing was amiss, but she was kept silent by the tremor in Mary's hand, by the redness that rimmed her eyes. What would she have said, anyway? That she had never left the lake? That she could swear she could hear water rushing in her ears, even now?

Sara followed Annaleigh and William through every room in the house, staying hidden in the shadows as Mary tried to keep herself occupied and distracted by directing the hired workers who were deconstructing what was left of the wedding ceremony. Flowers were whisked away on trucks, instructed to be laid on any empty grave in the cemetery. The leftover food was packaged and donated to the orphanage in town. Annaleigh hadn't noticed the charitable side of Mary before, but she realized now that it had always been there. She did not order excess for her parties out of vanity but in the anticipation of surplus food untouched by the guests who attended.

Mary was always doing small things to make the lives of other people easier. She noticed the preciousness of life, saw how easily it could be yanked out from under a person. It couldn't have been easy to see the future and not be able to do anything about it; it must have been even harder to look into the faces of the dead and only be able to answer them in whispers. She'd become a practiced liar, indeed.

Annaleigh couldn't stand to live inside her skin. Yet she managed. The morning came and went at an agonizing pace, but the pain—the heat she felt at every point of contact—was getting easier to bear. By the afternoon, the fire at her back had dulled to a slight sting, reminding her of a particularly bad sunburn she'd gotten one summer down by the lake.

The lake…

She kept going to the windows and searching the shore for herself, wondering when she would wash up. Just before dinner, she thought she had seen something. It was a tangle of white, the fabric paled to semi-transparency from the water.

"Mary—" Annaleigh said. She'd tried to keep her voice to a calm whisper, but she could feel the hysteria that had sneaked through.

William followed Mary when she ran to join her by the window. Sara waited behind them, wanting to reach out to touch William's shoulder but denying herself the satisfaction. He still had the locket, kept it safe in his pocket. As long as he kept it with him, he would be able to see all that Mary could. Sara had to stay hidden; Annaleigh had to stay visible.

"Mary," Annaleigh whispered, quieter still. "That's not…"

"No," Mary said. "God, no. They're the linens that were taken down to the water for a good scrubbing."

"Whatever did you think they were?" William asked, pushing back the curtain to get a better look.

"N-nothing." Annaleigh found another smile within her to ease his worry. "Of course it is the linens."

The rest of the afternoon was quiet and strained. Mary and Annaleigh tried to keep some level of easy conversation going, though it was forced and tiresome.

The conversation only lulled once, when Mary's eyes glazed over for the ghost of a second. When she came to again, she was shaking, her fingers twitching with the fabric of her dress, picking at the pillows on the couch. She couldn't quite meet Annaleigh's gaze after that, but she continued to lob bits of chatter to her, anything to keep up the ruse that everything was fine.

William didn't notice the tremor in her voice, but Annaleigh could practically feel the alarm vibrating off of her. She pretended she didn't; there was a lot of pretending that night. They exchanged furtive glances to William, but he never showed any signs of suspicion that something was off. Not until Annaleigh made her first mistake.

"What book are you reading?" Annaleigh asked him.

"See for yourself," he said, closing the book and tossing it across the room to her.

The cover fluttered open as the book spun toward her. She reached out a hand to catch it, but Mary made a sound—too quiet for William to hear. Annaleigh had heard, though, and noticed the dread that widened her eyes. She didn't have time to interpret its meaning, and before she could react, the book passed through her hand and slid across the floor behind her.

"I thought you had it...?" William sat up from the couch, looking around the floor for where the book had landed. "It looked like you had it. You never drop books."

She couldn't hear him. She was too busy flexing her fingers in wonder, in terror. The insubstantial feeling she'd had before swamped her in fear. It was becoming her, and she was...unbecoming. She could feel it. The line to the anchor had snapped, and her life before had officially drifted out of reach, a flower floating across the water.

There was nothing Annaleigh feared more than oblivion. The one thing she had truly been fearful of in life was death—not the possible pain or sadness, though that was something horrid in itself, but the idea of one day not *being* anymore. That she would be gone, buried, and forgotten. This was worse. She was vanishing from the world, but no one realized it.

No one but Mary. Mary could see the change, the slight sparkle around Annaleigh's silhouette, the translucency in her coloring. Annaleigh appeared to be stitched to this world by a thread of stars, but it wasn't enough to hold her true. She was a fading photograph, and if one were to look closely enough, they would notice the visibility of the furniture behind her, the curve of the back of the patterned couch just under her pointed shoulders.

William got up, moving to Annaleigh. Sara appeared in the doorway behind him, panicked. Mary acted before she had time to think, knocking over a lamp. It fell to the ground and its globe shattered.

"Mary!" William stopped where he stood, barefoot and surrounded by dangerous shards of broken glass. "What the hell was that?"

"Sorry," Mary said. "Anna, you're closest to the door, would you be a dear and grab someone to clean this up before Will tries to walk across it?" She turned to Annaleigh and sent a silent message through her eyes, a warning to leave, to focus her energy enough to look real again. "The last thing I need tonight is to stitch up Will's feet."

Without a word, Annaleigh ran from the room, Sara on her heels.

When she was out in the hall, she heard Mary call after her. "Don't mind sending anyone after all. I've found a pan!"

Annaleigh leaned in a doorway farther down the dark hall. The light shrank away from her, skirting just to her toes and then bowing back, as if it were afraid to get too near. "I'm disappearing."

"I know, sweet girl. I know. It's awful," Sara said.

She nodded. "I... How can I keep this up like this?" She motioned to herself, and when she looked down, she could only see shadows. They had swallowed her up and rebuilt her, made her a part of them.

"It won't be much longer. I promise. This part gets easier. You can learn to control it with focus."

"And the other parts?" Annaleigh said.

She pushed herself from the wall to face Sara better. It took all the restraint she had to keep from crying again. She'd had enough of tears.

"The part where every inch of me *aches* to be alive again?" she asked Sara, her voice cracking. "The part where I wish I could just rest, be done with this life that I no longer own? Or what about the part where I want to scream and tell William everything? How it makes my heart break every time I look at his face and lie to him."

"You're not lying—"

"My entire *existence* is a lie." Annaleigh squared her shoulders. "I'm on stolen time, and I don't know how much longer I have. I don't know how much longer I *want* to have." She needed a fight, wanted someone to blame or yell at for what had happened to her. But as she looked over Sara and saw the sincere grief and regret that lowered her chin and weighed down her shoulders, the anger drained from her. It pooled at her feet and cooled into fear. The anger was easier to deal with than this dread. "I'm scared. I'm so scared of what will happen next."

Sara could say nothing of comfort, but she touched her, and that was enough. It had to be enough. It was a mother's touch, a soft caress of her cheek and brush of her hair, a gentle hug and kiss laid on the top of her head.

"Will anyone ever find me?" Annaleigh asked.

From the golden room behind her, she heard Mary curse. "Your *feet*, Will!"

William crashed out into the hallway, his hair mussed from his fidgety hands, the legs of his pants cuffed above his ankles, and his feet bleeding. He was laughing to himself, looking back into the room at Mary, but when he spun around and looked down the hallway, he froze. He could have sworn to himself that he had seen—

Sara let the shadows consume her.

"Who were you talking to?" he asked Annaleigh, walking over to her on his heels.

"You're bleeding," Annaleigh said.

"Were you just talking to—"

"Myself," she said, waving away his question as she bent down to her knees. "Just myself. You're bleeding."

He looked down the hallway past Annaleigh for a moment before answering. "Mary was picking up the pieces too slowly."

"So you walked across the glass barefoot?"

"I think she did it on purpose. Going at such a lazy pace just to bother me."

Mary called from the room, "I can hear you."

"Yes, well, good then," William said with a smirk to Annaleigh.

She smiled, forgetting for a moment how she was being washed out of this world. The remembering came slamming back into her and she looked away, bending to her knees to instead focus on picking out the small shards of glass he had brought into the dark hallway with him.

"Do you need light?" William asked.

"No," Annaleigh answered before he had a chance to strike one of the matches he kept in his back pocket.

It took all of her energy to focus on feeling real, on making her fingers solid enough to touch him and not reach right through him to the floor. When Mary finally emerged from the room, she brought a roll of gauze and set about bandaging his foot.

"I'm not a child," William said.

"Then don't act like one," Mary said. "Walking across a room of glass like some insolent toddler." She clicked her tongue. Her hands were focused on the task of cleaning up and bandaging his foot, but her eyes were studying Annaleigh. "You should go to bed now before you end up causing more trouble."

"If I recall, *I* wasn't the one who broke the lamp or dropped the book," he said, leaning his shoulder against the wall and abandoning any hope of salvaging his dignity.

"It's been a long day, Will," Mary said. "We should all get some rest."

"I'm exhausted," Annaleigh added. "Let's go to bed, William."

Mary pulled out some small scissors and snipped the last of the gauze. "Doctor's orders," she said. "Now go up to bed."

William took Annaleigh's hand and they made their way upstairs. Annaleigh's vision darkened, like she was going to faint again, but it was a different kind of buzzing in her head. It was the sapping of energy, the fatigue of focus. It took so much effort to feel real, to exist for him, that she was sure she would evaporate into thin air if she stopped thinking about it even for just a moment.

"Anna, wait," Mary said.

William let go of Annaleigh's hand but remained at the banister as Mary met her halfway up the winding staircase.

"No, you go, Will. Get in bed before you bleed out in the hallway," Mary said.

"Talking about me?" William asked suspiciously.

"We have more stimulating conversation topics than you, *William*," Mary said. "But if it would help inflate your ego further, go ahead and believe that."

With a laugh and a slow shake of his head, he drew down the hallway and into his room, closing the door behind him.

Mary waited several breaths before she said anything, and when she did, she spoke in rushed whispers. "I saw something…"

Annaleigh shook her head, confused. "Something more? I'm already dead, Mary." The word *dead* stuck to her tongue like paper. "What more could go wrong?"

Sara joined them, keeping close to the wall in case William peeked his head out again. If he thought he saw her twice, it would be too much to explain away.

"Your body…" Mary looked green even in the darkness. She was shaky and her skin had the light sheen of sweat. Her lips wobbled over at least a dozen sentences before she could find anything to say out loud. "I had another vision. You—your *body*. It surfaces."

Now Annaleigh felt ill. Her knees weakened beneath her, and she wondered if she fell, would she make any sound? Or would she fall right through the floorboards and sink all the way down to the cool stone of the basement?

"When?" Sara asked.

"You don't know?" Mary said, angry, defeated. "You can see what happens too, you know. This doesn't have to all be on my shoulders."

"I can't see like you, Mary," Sara said. "I see only what I'm allowed."

"Soon. Tomorrow, maybe? I'm not sure. It's hard to tell." Mary shook her head. "It's not like it comes with a written time. No one tells me *when* it's going to happen. I don't get an RSVP."

Annaleigh gripped the polished railing. "What did I look like?"

"Anna—"

"Did I look... Were my eyes open?"

"It may be best not to know, Annaleigh," Sara said gently. "The unpleasantness of it could be enough to undo you entirely."

"I'm already undone," Annaleigh said. "I'm dead, and I'm talking to another ghost, but Mary and William can still see me. I don't think knowing the last image of myself would be what tips me over into hysterics."

"They closed your eyes," Mary finally said.

What she didn't tell her was how pale and bleary they were before the police shut them for her. She didn't mention the blueness of her skin, the darkness of her lips—purple, like two violet petals resting in snow. She didn't want to tell her that the flowers she had put in her braids for the wedding had fallen out and tangled in her stringy, knotted hair. She didn't want her to picture how tiny she looked in her heavy, white wedding dress or how it took five men to pull her to shore. How her father had been one of them...

"You and Will need to leave," Mary said. "He can't see this. Tomorrow afternoon, I'll arrange a carriage. It'll be your...your honeymoon." The word was sour in her mouth, like curdled milk. "You have to get him away from here."

"Annaleigh..." Sara began, but the bedroom door upstairs cracked open.

"Mary, stop pestering Annaleigh with whatever you've concocted now," William called down. "It can wait until morning."

"I'm not *pestering* her, Will," Mary said, bringing out the usual tone she used with him. Teasing, lighthearted. Nothing like the heavy somberness she kept on her face. She was allowed to grieve in the darkness, at least.

"All the same, I'd love to see my wife."

"I'll be right there," Annaleigh said, her voice as thin as she felt.

The door closed again, and the psychic and two specters on the steps listened to his footsteps across the room until they heard the creak of his bed frame and the whisper of his sheets.

"Tomorrow afternoon," Mary repeated. "Far from here."

Annaleigh nodded and climbed back up the stairs, leaving the truth behind her to live another night as a liar. She went to William's room, shut the door, and climbed into the darkness with him. He wrapped her in his arms, and there was nothing she wanted more than to get lost in him, but she was all too aware of fading away.

She was an apparition, as brilliant and shimmery as a hallucination. For the first time since his wedding night, William noticed the paranormal beauty, the strangeness of her being. The moonlight slid through her as if she weren't even there. Even though her head lay upon his chest, her hand on his stomach, he was the only one bathed in moonlight. But he was tired, and he had always believed she had been crafted by the moon. Only the mirage of his dream allowed him to see the truth in that sentiment. Or that's what he told himself.

CHAPTER 14

A Commotion

"BUT WHERE EXACTLY ARE WE going?" William asked at breakfast, stacking his plate as high as he could with eggs. He was eating enough to not realize that everyone else's settings sat empty before them.

"The mountains." Mary stood with her clean plate and stared out the tall windows. It was a gray morning, and the sky was heavy with the warning of a storm. She hoped the worst of it would hold off until the evening or the roads would be impossible to travel.

"The mountains?"

"I've never been to the mountains, William," Annaleigh said, covering her plate with a cloth napkin. "But from everything Mary's told me, it is beautiful up there."

"It is," Mary assured her. "Very far away from everything." She glanced over her shoulder at Annaleigh. "It's like living in a world devoid of crowds and noise."

"Do I have a choice in the matter?" William asked.

"No," the girls answered together.

"Besides, Will, it'll be good to get away. You haven't been to the mountains since—" *Before mother died.* The words silently dropped from Mary's mouth.

Before. That's how William marked his life. Before his mother had passed and after. He didn't know that she was still there, following him and watching as he grew into the man he'd become. Now that Annaleigh had joined his mother on the list of loves he'd lost, how would he measure his time? Would there be two befores, two afters? Or would one take precedence?

"The carriage arrives after lunch. You'll be there by the evening if this storm holds off." She leaned closer to the window, brushing the curtain out of the way with the back of her hand.

William left his breakfast and joined her at the window. They squinted at the sky, and in the reflection of the glass, Annaleigh could see how strikingly similar they appeared. They both had the same wrinkle on their nose when they tried to see something very far away, and that raven hair of theirs…

"Their father couldn't stand it," Sara said from beside Annaleigh. She kept her voice nearly silent as Mary and William bickered about the weather.

"They look so much like you," Annaleigh said. "It would have broken his heart every day to look at them and see you. That's no way for a father to be with their children. Physically there, but mentally gone. It's better he's entirely gone."

Sara considered her. "You're wiser than your years, Anna."

"I guess I have to be. I didn't have the luxury of many years to grow into my cleverness."

"No, you didn't." She laid her hand upon hers and squeezed gently. "I'm so sorry."

Neither of them had to focus on being real, on being whole, with one another. It was easier to be transitory and insubstantial. The effort of existing in a world she didn't belong in was too great.

"It's nothing," Mary said from the window, her voice sounding panicked. She tried to close the curtains, but William wouldn't allow it. "Will, would you please? It's nothing of our concern. Let's go get you both packed for your trip—"

"Mary, let me see!" He moved her out of the way, pushing open the curtains as wide as they would go.

Sara looked up at Mary and they met eyes. The word *help* formed on Mary's lips, and before she could say anything else, Sara had left the room, her movements stiff with concern. William looked back at the table, empty save for Annaleigh's small frame in a wide, oak chair.

"There's something happening at the lake," he said. "Come have a look. There's a large crowd gathered. Some shouting…" He looked back down their lawn and screwed up his eyes in an attempt to get a better look at the commotion. "Is that Officer Harley?"

"No, Will. Just go pack your things, will you please?" Mary begged. "If you are late in leaving, you'll be stuck on the side of the road in this storm!"

"It doesn't look like it will rain. The clouds are heavy with threat, not promise," William said, but just as the last words left his mouth, rain tapped on the window, tiny fingers teasing him from the other side of the pane. "Or we'll just wait until tomorrow."

"William…" Annaleigh stood up, uneasy on her feet. Her stomach felt like it had been tied in a delicate bow, and she could feel the angry squeeze of a suffocating corset though she wasn't wearing one. The world rocked below her, and everything felt too hot again. "I don't feel so well." She hadn't meant to say it out loud, but she was so focused on staying solid and real that she'd forgotten to keep track of her mouth.

William turned from the window and Mary snatched the curtains closed immediately.

"Take her upstairs to lie down, Will," Mary told him, "or neither of you will be leaving tonight."

"What's wrong?" He rushed over to her and grabbed her hand, having her sit again. She couldn't hide her shudder when he touched her, couldn't pretend to be fine to ease the worry that tangled his brows. "Do you need a doctor? I thought I saw Dr. Borough down at the lake. Let me fetch him for you."

"No," Mary and Annaleigh answered together. They exchanged a fearful look.

"What was that?" William asked, looking between the two. "What are you hiding?"

"Nothing," Annaleigh said. "I just… I don't need a doctor. I'm just lightheaded. I think it's still the exhaustion."

"I'll get you a glass of water," Mary said, rushing out of the room the same way Sara had gone.

"And I'm getting you a doctor. I won't have my wife gritting her teeth in pain to just get through the day."

He stood to leave, grabbing his coat from the back of his chair and spinning it onto himself. An image of him in that very same coat, proposing, popped into her head again, though his pocket had been stuffed with a ring box instead of his fist.

"No, William," Annaleigh said, standing and following him out into the foyer.

"Wait here. I'll be back before you know it. Where is Mary with that water?" He opened the door and pushed his way out into the rain.

The sky was at the precipice of a great storm. The clouds above were thick and gray, and Annaleigh felt that they existed more truly than she did. They felt more real and substantial than she ever would again, and she wanted to scream. Lightning peeled across the sky, followed shortly after by a roll of thunder that rattled her soul.

She hesitated in the doorway, flooded with memories of the past and worries about the future. She wanted to follow him into the rain, but something stopped her. As William made his way down the front path to the hillside above the lake, she froze, wondering if the rain would fall right through her.

"Mary," she called behind her. Terror shaped her words and raised her voice an octave. "Mary!"

She appeared at the top of the steps with Sara, eyes wide. Annaleigh could swear she heard her stuttering heartbeat through the roar of the rain as it fell heavier outside.

"He's gone," Annaleigh said. The words broke her, but she managed to stay standing.

"*Merde*." Mary came flying down the stairs and charging out into the torrent of rain without even grabbing her coat.

Sara stopped next to Annaleigh and touched her back gently. "You have to go after him. He cannot see—"

"I can't. I can't…"

"You must."

Annaleigh had very little faith in the strength fate believed she possessed. She wasn't sure how to save someone when she wasn't even able to save herself. There were no words to console someone who was bereft of the person consoling them. She made no sense in destiny's plan. But she didn't need to believe in herself to charge into the rain. She didn't need courage to follow after Mary and rush to William. She only needed fear. The fear of what would happen if she *didn't*.

The rain answered her question of how it would greet her: with indifference. It paid her no mind as she stood facing William, scrambling together a sentence to persuade him to go back inside. She would have slammed into his back if she were corporeal, but instead, she ran through him, her shoulder breaking over his like smoke. She twisted around in front of him, doing all she could to look solid and block his view.

"Annaleigh, I told you to wait."

"I'm feeling much better," she said, forcing a smile that might have looked a bit manic.

"You're going to catch a cold, and then you *won't* be feeling much better," he said, taking off his coat to give to her.

Before he placed it on her shoulders, she stepped back, worried it would go right through her and land in the wet grass beneath their feet. He held it out to her for a moment before she shook her head.

"Will!" Mary's voice carried loud across the hillside.

He spun around to her. "Are you both *mad*?"

"Let's go back inside," Annaleigh said. "Really, I'm fine. I'll take a warm bath, and we will pack, and then we can leave. The roads shouldn't be too bad, and if they are, it'll just be a longer journey. I want you to show me the mountains."

"Will!" Mary was panting by the time she caught up with them.

He shook his head. "Why on earth —"

"Don't go down there," Mary said. Her hair was a wet, tangled mess, making Annaleigh's appearance even stranger. Not a single drop of rain had touched her, but William had yet to notice.

"The lake?" he asked, raising a suspicious eyebrow. "Why not? What's happening?"

Annaleigh shook her head and Mary just mumbled, "Nothing."

"What has gotten into the two of you?" He watched them, waiting for an answer, but they had none to offer. "Right. Then you two go back inside and get out of the rain, and I'm going to go see what all the commotion is down here."

Mary grabbed his arm, and Annaleigh shifted back to block him from going any farther.

"Will you both calm down?" William said, shaking off Mary and sidestepping Annaleigh. He continued down the slippery hill, squelching in the mud. "That lake is half on our property, and if anything is wrong down there, we should know."

Mary sped her pace. "I'll check, Will. I will see what is happening and report back to you and Anna, and then you can go to the mountains."

"Mary." His voice was warning.

"Let me go see, okay? Take Anna back to the house."

"I should be the one to talk to Officer Harley. He knows me," William said.

"He knows me too," Mary countered. "Please, just—"

"Mary, stop." He pushed faster down to the shore of the lake, skirting the crowd with Mary close at his heel, still urging him home. But her pleads only piqued his curiosity.

Annaleigh felt her limbs stiffen with a cold, creeping feeling. She didn't want to go any farther, didn't want to see herself bloated and blue. But she couldn't stop moving. Even as her head was begging for her to stop, to turn away, she kept on. She wove through the bodies of people who had just days ago sat at this very lake and watched her marry. No one turned to her; no one saw her. When she bumped into someone's shoulder, they turned and their gaze slid past her.

It was a horrible feeling, being looked at but not seen. But it got so much worse…

She heard her father shouting, her mother sobbing, and if she still had blood running through her, she would have felt it turn to ice. Ahead, Mary tugged at William's hand, trying to slow him down. But he pressed forward faster, hearing the familiar voices drenched in grief.

Mary pulled as hard as she could at her brother, pleading for him to stop. Annaleigh felt herself shrinking until she felt as invisible as she appeared to everyone else. There were hushed

120

whispers around her, whispers that silenced and then crescendoed as William passed, Mary toting along behind him.

Heat rose in Annaleigh's face, a panicked feeling that sang in her gut and seared up to her temples. She could scream and cry and fly away on the whispers of the crowd, but she couldn't do anything when everything went still and very, very quiet.

$\mathscr{Part}$ 4

The angels, not half so happy in Heaven,
Went envying her and me—
Yes!—that was the reason (as all men know,
In this kingdom by the sea)
That the wind came out of the cloud by night,
Chilling and killing my Annabel Lee.

— Stanza IV, *Annabel Lee* by Edgar Allan Poe

CHAPTER 15

The Shore

MARY SMACKED INTO WILLIAM'S BACK, right between his shoulder blades. She didn't even realize they had made it through the thick huddle of people. They had emerged from the press of bodies and whispers and stood on the edge—the edge of the crowd, the edge of the world... Wherever they were, she felt they were falling. They were falling as fast as the rain.

William was frozen, and Mary could feel his heartbeat through his back. She wanted to stay hidden behind him, cowering like a child from the terrible tableau before them, but she couldn't let him take the brunt of this pain. Not on his own.

She moved next to him, saw Annaleigh tiptoe around both of them and conceal herself in the woods. The pale dress she was wearing flitted behind the knots of shrubbery that bunched around the roots of the trees. Mary didn't want William to see this scene, but she didn't want Annaleigh to see it either. From her vision in her dream, she knew it would be too much for either of them to bear.

"Will," she said, tugging at his arm. "We need to go home."

"Impossible," was all he said. He took a tentative step forward and then several back. The crowd spread around him like a ripple, giving him room to collapse, but he stayed on his feet. "*Impossible,*" he said again.

"Will," Mary whispered in his ear, trying to pull him back from the brink of insanity. "*I can explain,* but we need to go home. Now."

"You can explain?" He didn't sound angry, only confused. Very, very confused and torn to shreds. "But she's right —"

William looked back to where Annaleigh had been standing, but she was gone. Water slid down his face and fell in his eyes, and he thought she must have been lost in the crowd behind them, the crowd of blotchy skin, wide eyes, and shocked faces. But then he turned back to the lake and saw her there on the sand. Blinking wouldn't vanish the image. Not believing it wouldn't make it all disappear. Annaleigh was there, on the shore, partially covered by a white sheet that had become translucent in the furious rain.

Even from this far away, William could see how cold she looked. She was blue. She was blue and fragile and impossible because he had just had breakfast with her, and she hadn't been out of his sight since... Since she'd almost drowned. Since she'd almost become this.

He shook the *almost* out of his head and could feel what was left of his logic spilling down his face in tears.

"No," was all he said, all he could manage. "No," was all he said a dozen times.

He took stuttering steps toward her, but the uniformed officers held him back. Dr. Borough was kneeling next to her — to her body — and looked up at William with sadness. Mary tried to pull William away, take him out of the straining arms of the officers, but he fought hard. He tried to break through them, calling her name over and over again.

126

"Annaleigh!"

Mary had broken down in tears behind him and they passed their pain back and forth through heaves and sobs.

Peering through the woods, Annaleigh watched everything collapse in front of her. She saw the people she knew in the crowds and their wet faces, the tracks of their tears obscured by the relentless rain. She watched as her mother was comforted by several women from town, all of whom were trying to tear her away from the scene. Her father broke her heart in a way she hadn't expected when she saw him fall to his knees and shout at the clouds that ripped open above him with tears of their own.

Carefully, she stepped through the woods, closer to herself—or what was left of her. She walked by her mother, brushing her hand over hers as she passed, and then her father. She bent down to kiss him once on the forehead before she left him to his grief. And then she sat down next to her body, crossed her legs, and touched her own cold, clammy face. It didn't feel real under her fingertips. She felt polished and waxy.

Mary had been right. They had closed her eyes and pulled a simple sheet over her. It was up to her shoulders, her face revealed for proper identification from her family, but the great skirts of her wedding dress that spilled out below the sheet were unmistakable.

William looked up from his broken sobs and watched. His mind fought with sense as he saw the twinning image of his wife, his Annaleigh—alive and very dead—in front of him. Looking up from her own body, Annaleigh caught his eye, and he finally noticed the *wrong*.

She had a gauzy appearance to her, like she was swathed in a sheer curtain. Like her veil was still pulled over her face. The rain had not touched her once. The body on the shore—*her body*, the acid churning in his stomach reminded him—was soaked and water puddled around it—*her*. But there she sat, looking at him through the rain, dry and perfect.

"*Impossible*," he said again.

His knees gave out beneath him, and Mary clung to him as best she could as he fell to the ground. The wetness of the sand seeped through to his knees, and he distantly heard Annaleigh's father asking questions, the police attempting to pacify his temper.

"How didn't he know? How couldn't he have known?" Annaleigh's father screamed, the grief melting into rage.

"Please!" Mary shouted back. "We thought she had gone to visit you, to pack the last of her things and say goodbye. She was due to return today to leave on their honeymoon."

Annaleigh's mother broke from the gaggle of women that had surrounded her to comfort her husband and cry on his shoulder. "Of course he didn't know. Look at him. *Look*."

Her father did look, but William could only stare back at his hands. He didn't want to see the double image of Annaleigh— the picture of her alive juxtaposed so violently with her lifeless form on the shore.

He was going to be sick. Breakfast came back to him in a wave of nausea, but he didn't allow himself to turn inside out. Not in front of everyone.

"He loved nothing more than her," Annaleigh's mother kept on, her sobs quieting. "He may have loved her more than we did."

"He did," Mary said.

"He does," whispered Annaleigh.

William couldn't hold his breakfast anymore.

CHAPTER 16

The Impossible

IT TOOK HOURS FOR THE crowds to disperse. In small groups, people left in whispers of apologies and quiet tears, but William didn't move. The rain had grown angrier before lightening to a sprinkling and then lifting altogether. Even after Annaleigh's mother and father had been escorted back to their home by a young officer, William remained. Just he, Mary, the doctor, and the dark clouds stayed on the shore.

William couldn't move from his knees, just feet away from his dead wife.

"How are you here?" he whispered to Annaleigh.

Doctor Boroughs looked up, confused. "We were called, son. One of the boys in town had seen something floating. Her dress…"

Her dress. He wanted to yell, to let the everything he felt claw its way out of his throat, but he felt too dead and hollow to find a big enough voice to do so.

"How long?" William asked.

The doctor pulled the sheet up to cover her face. "More than a day. She's still in her wedding dress, so I'd assume—"

The doctor's voice droned on as Annaleigh tilted her head and clenched her hands together in fists. "I never surfaced."

"She never surfaced..." William repeated to himself, to the sand under his knees.

"I'm afraid not," said Doctor Boroughs.

"How is that possible?" William dug his fingers into the ground, let the uncomfortable feeling of the grit under his fingernails distract him from the severe pain of looking at his Annaleigh, drowned—and somehow alive. Was she alive? "She's dead," he said to himself. He said it over and over again, trying to let its truth sink into his skin. But it wouldn't, because there she was. Watching him. Watching him watch her. How was she there?

"The weight of her wedding dress," Doctor Boroughs explained, "was considerable. She didn't have a chance."

It was the wrong thing to say to him. William bent over, tearing at the ground, heaving and gagging on the nothing in his stomach. Mary set her hand on his back as he tried in vain to expel the sickness inside him.

He had to be mad. Her body lay right in front of him— undeniable proof that she was dead. That she had really drowned, that he hadn't saved her from the lake that night. *She didn't have a chance*.

The doctor gave a signal and a few more men emerged. They placed a stretcher down next to her and moved her body with great care, but it still seemed too rough to William. He saw her head bounce on the fabric stretched between the two poles they lifted, grew sick when he saw the train of her wedding dress trailing behind her as they carried her away. And then he was alone, with Mary and a ghost.

"This is my fault," he said.

"No," Mary said, angry.

Annaleigh didn't move from where she was sitting, from here she had last seen her body. She wondered where they would put it. In the mausoleum the Calloways owned? Or in a simple grave where her mother and father were supposed to be buried?

"I was the one who told her to meet me here," William argued back.

Most people were desperate to spread the blame to someone else, to pass on the gnawing feeling of guilt. Not William—he harbored the hate his father had toward him, a strong detestation for his own self.

"I told you," he said to Annaleigh. "I said five minutes. I promised."

Annaleigh remembered his lips at her ear, laughing at her urgency for him to meet her.

"I was late. Six minutes," he said. "That one minute—"

"Wouldn't have changed a damn thing, and you know it," Mary said.

He turned to his sister, his eyes wrecked. He needed her to understand. "She wouldn't have been anywhere near the lake if I hadn't suggested it!"

"Yes, I would have," Annaleigh said. Her voice was quiet, and he heard the delicacy in it now. There were so many things he noticed about her now that it was too late. "I was the one who wanted the ceremony at the lake. I was the one who needed to get air. I would have made my way down to the lake regardless if you had suggested it, and I was the one who dropped the locket and almost lost it."

William pulled the locket out from his pocket. "This locket?" He looked at it like a hated, cursed thing. "Christ, I want nothing to do with this thing. It has brought me nothing but pain, nothing but torment."

He pulled back his arm and tossed the locket as far away from him as he could. The chain flew through the air and the locket disappeared into the gnarled trees of the woods. He looked back over to Annaleigh, but she was gone. Panicked, he searched down the shore for where she had disappeared to, tossed his head back and forth to find where she had gone.

She was nowhere.

"Annaleigh?" Her name was soft on his lips, and he staggered to his feet. He stumbled drunkenly to where she had been sitting, but his mind was more sober than he could stand. "Annaleigh?" he called, his voice shredded, in ribbons.

Mary stood with him, grabbing her arm. "She's here. She's not gone."

"Where is she?"

Annaleigh rose and went to him, wanting nothing more than to silent the fevered fear she heard in his voice. She let her hand rest on his cheek, but he looked right through her. She kissed his cheek, but he turned away from her, his eyes still searching.

"I'm here. I'm here. Mary, why can't he see that I'm here?"

Mary cursed under her breath and looked to the woods. "The locket."

"What about the locket?" William asked, following her gaze.

"That's how you can see her. The only way…"

"But you can see her?"

Mary nodded.

"Now?" William clarified. "Without the locket?"

Mary nodded again. "I can see…a lot…without the locket."

William put his hands to his temples. It was too much too soon, and he couldn't stand any more life-altering news. He didn't want to hear more secrets he couldn't stand. He didn't want to hear the truth anymore. He preferred living in the bliss of lies.

He ran into the woods, searching through the brush for the golden locket. It was hanging off a spare spindle of a branch, swinging back and forth in a hypnotic rhythm. He grabbed it, turned back to the shore, and nearly ran straight into Annaleigh. She had been standing inches from him, invisible but ever-present.

"Anna." He choked on her name. "Annaleigh..." His fingers twitched to reach out and touch her, but he was worried about what would meet him, what wouldn't meet him. "I want to touch you. I want you to be real."

"I am real," she said, stepping closer and placing her hand on him. He could feel the coldness of her hand, and he wondered how he had ever believed he'd saved her from the ice of the lake.

"No you're not." The realization made his heart feel too small in his chest. "You're dead," he whispered. "*Dead*." He was carved out, emptied, and refilled with something that didn't belong to him.

"I'm here. I'm here, with you and Mary. And Sara."

"Sara...as in, my *mother?*"

Annaleigh stepped back from him and held out her hand. "Please, let's go home. Mary can explain better than I."

William didn't take her hand, but he followed her out of the woods. He avoided looking at the impression in the sand where her body had lain, he tried as best he could to not check if she was making footprints now, and he tried to not go insane in the sudden silence of his mind as he walked back to his haunted house with his sister who could see the impossible and his impossible wife.

CHAPTER 17

The Explanation

SAMUEL MET MARY AND WILLIAM at the door and nearly closed it on Annaleigh, but she managed to squeeze through at the last second. He led them to the front parlor and took away William's coat without a word, leaving them alone, cold, and heavy with rainwater and tension.

Annaleigh paced by the windows and the gray light of outside shone through her. William had to turn away before he collapsed. Instead, he faced Mary, waiting for an explanation — not that any she would deliver would help him in even the smallest way.

It took her an eternity to find the right words, but when Mary finally spoke, she did so in a whisper. Still, her secrets echoed. "I can see...*things.*"

"Things?" William asked, running his shaking hand over his face. He hadn't expected her to start with that. He wanted to know what had happened to Annaleigh, what was happening to him, why he could see someone who was dead. Someone who had drowned and never surfaced, yet there she stood just a few paces behind him.

He wanted to know why. He wanted to know how.

He wanted to unknow everything he had seen that morning.

More than anything, he wanted to rebel against the thought—the chance, the idea, the possibility—that Annaleigh was gone. That he'd left her in the lake that night, that he'd swum to the surface alone. He couldn't believe that something so unthinkable could happen, couldn't believe that there would be a world without her. The planets would have fallen out of the sky if she were gone.

That's the universe he existed in: the one with her. Where did he exist now? Where did *she*?

But how could he fight the truth? How could he have ever thought that she'd survived after seeing her there on the shore, looking so lost. So small. So lifeless.

"People, shadows," Mary went on. She spoke in a rushed manner, using wild hand gestures that told of her agitation. "Visions—dreams that come true. It's not always coherent." She cleared her throat and looked at Annaleigh then immediately at her feet. "I can't stop what I see from happening."

William gripped the back of the couch he stood behind to steady himself. He dug his fingers into the fabric, grasping at the last threads of his sanity he felt were wearing thin. "You can see...people."

"Who have died but not yet left. That's how I knew about mother before you told me," Mary said.

Annaleigh stopped pacing and stood in the dark corner of the room, watching the two siblings. A scene from the past played before her eyes. They'd been in this very room, standing in nearly these very spots, coping with a different loss.

After the night at the lake when William had cried over his mother and thrown his father's letter into the lake, Annaleigh had helped him home to deliver news no brother should ever have to hand down to his younger sister. Mary had been twelve, but she'd looked no older than ten—small and pale with eyes too big for her face.

Annaleigh held William's hand as he repeated the contents of his father's letter to Mary, told her about their mother passing away. They had expected tears from Mary, some kind of tantrum denying that it was even *possible* their mother—who had been so young and perfect and healthy—was dead. She didn't cry though. She only moved over on the couch and stared at the air next to her in wonder.

Then she stood up, crossed the room, and dragged William into a hug he returned stiffly with shock. "She's fine, Will. Mother will never leave us."

A few weeks later, when Sara's belongings arrived in the post, Mary took out her locket, polished it, and kept it safe in her jewelry box to one day find a new purpose.

Looking back at that day. knowing what she knew now about Mary, she found that her reaction made sense. The sparkle in Mary's eye had been too bright to be grief, and it'd looked *so much* as though she were sharing the couch with some invisible person.

William's voice scattered the memory like a hand batting away smoke. "You saw her."

"*See* her," Mary corrected.

"That's not—" He gasped, the air knocked from him. "That's not possible. This isn't real."

Annaleigh stepped up behind William to rest her hand on his back as Sara came into the room. It was too much for William though. He was bookended by ghosts, and he was spent, exhausted by the impossibility of everything. Everything he saw was wrong.

He stepped away from Annaleigh—not sure he wanted her to touch him anymore, not sure he wanted her to stop touching him—and sank to the couch. Sara kept her distance as if she were ready to disappear into the shadows of the hallway beyond the room if he told her to go.

But he didn't tell her to go. He couldn't tell either of his haunts to leave him to his peace, because he wasn't sure he deserved it.

It was a peculiar kind of torture, living beside the dead. There was no future here, only past. It was living in a memory and never wanting to acknowledge the present that was so empty now that they had gone. But they hadn't gone. Not really. They remained, watching him, and all he could do was watch them back.

"My son," Sara said. Still, she did not move. "You deserve so much more than this life of pain you've been dealt."

He put his head in his hands at the sound of her voice. He could have pretended that Mary had been lying to him before — convinced himself that Annaleigh was a delusion he'd invented for himself because he'd blocked the truth of that night, that he'd never saved her. But then Sara's voice…

It was agonizing to see her, to hear that voice of his mother, the voice he had heard nearly every night in his dreams since she'd left him as a child. It was a pain that lit him from inside, like the burn of drinking tea too quickly but being greedy enough not to slow down. He wanted her to speak more, to never speak again.

How could something so unimaginable be real? How could the dead walk next to him, speak to him? How long had he been in the company of ghosts?

Mary was jumpy, nervous to be sharing the world she had always kept to herself with her brother, who was falling apart faster than she could fix him.

"It's not possible. How is this *possible*?" he asked the blackness behind his eyes. It was the same thought that kept snagging in his mind. It tore him to shreds as he sat there, in a room of phantoms. "I can't be here," he said suddenly, standing up. "I have to go. I need to get away from here, from this... all of it."

Annaleigh rocked back and forth on her toes, trying to reconcile the duality in her. She wanted to embrace him, to cry with him over the life they'd both lost. It was a selfish wish, a need for him to take away her pain and absorb it into himself, to tell her that everything would be all right even though nothing was the least bit right. It was all wrong, so wrong, and she could see what it was doing to him. He was unraveling, and she was the one pulling him apart. She would destroy him.

She needed to leave. Her absence would halve him, but he would heal. Her death was a laceration on his soul that needed to close and scar over, but as long as she was with him, twisting that dagger of her presence deeper, there would be no alleviation to his agony.

It was selfish to stay, but it was impossible to leave. She didn't think she would be able to leave even if she could—where would she go? How could she stop existing? Sara told her she wasn't finished with this life, that she still had much to do. But as she studied the broken curve of William's back, she felt that she had already done too much.

"Go?" Mary echoed.

William couldn't meet anyone's gaze. "I'll take the carriage you sent for, and I will leave. Alone."

"Will—" Mary's panic matched Annaleigh's.

Her decision had been made for her, then. He'd leave her and she'd let him. She would allow him to grieve far from her memory, from her residual presence.

He didn't look back as he left the room, rushed up to his room, and packed his things. He didn't even say goodbye when he ran outside and jumped into the carriage that had pulled up out front. But he did look out the window as it drove away, and he saw three figures watching as he left them behind.

As he rattled past the lake, he jumped out of the carriage. The driver pulled the horses to a stop as William collapsed into the mud and turned inside out one last time, choking on the acid of his stomach and the lies that sewed up his life. Wiping his mouth on his sleeve, he climbed back into the carriage and slumped on the velvet bench. He put his head in his hands and wished with every ounce of strength he had left that he had been just one minute earlier that night.

He never should have surfaced without her.

CHAPTER 18

The Tether

"MARY, I CAN'T LET HIM go," Annaleigh said, her voice shaking. She watched as the carriage grew smaller and smaller as it drove off the Calloway estate, tried to make sense of the smudges beyond the foggy window.

"He was in such pain," Sara said. Her hand came to a rest on Mary's shoulder. "Did you feel it?"

Mary grit her teeth. "Of course I felt it. I felt it twin with my own, a tangle of emotions so dark I thought…" She shook her head, stepped back from the window. "I will give him a few day's lead, and then I will follow after him. He cannot be alone for long."

"No," Annaleigh agreed. She pushed closer to the window as Mary and Sara stepped away. "He should never be alone."

She kept standing there, not wanting to close the curtains and accept that he was gone, hoping beyond hope that she'd see the carriage pull back into the courtyard. That he'd jump out and realize all wasn't lost. She wanted to pretend that nothing had changed for just a little longer, but she knew it was too late for that. It had always been too late.

Her head buzzed, the sound of a thousand flies disorienting her. She could see two worlds beyond the windows, bleary and confusing. It was as if she existed in two spaces, and she wasn't sure which she preferred. Mary and Sara's worried conversation was muffled behind her, but there was a creaking and the sound of hooves in mud.

Annaleigh thought the world below her was suddenly uneven and rocky. She felt like she was moving, and she could feel her stomach jostle as she slammed over a bump, but she was standing perfectly still at the window. The crying she heard, though, was all too real, and she could clearly smell the sharp, green scent of William.

"Mary?" She put her hand to her head.

Distantly, she thought Mary called after her, maybe even touched her, but in one slow blink, the house disappeared around her. The large room shrank close to her, closing her in on all sides. She was no longer standing on hardwood, but sitting on a velvet bench, looking across a dark, tottering cab at William.

He had his head in his hands, his elbows perched on his knees, and his breathing was loud and jagged, as if his lungs were snagging on his ribs. He removed one of the hands from his head and reached into his pocket to pull out the locket. It was small in his hands, and he turned it over again and again, rubbing his thumb across its filigree face. William didn't notice her presence, and she didn't want to scare him, but she couldn't help the gasp of surprise.

She hadn't meant to follow him.

He looked up to her, and she saw the flare of pain she brought to him.

"I didn't mean to," Annaleigh said, her voice dull in the small space of the carriage.

The carriage bounced on the rocky road beneath them, and she was bumped up on her seat and sent sprawling into the bench in front of her. She landed hard on her knees and slammed forward onto the empty spot of the bench William sat on. It hadn't hurt—nothing more than the burning pain of contact she had begun to grow accustomed to—but William reacted as though it had.

He reached to her, pocketing the locket. For a moment, he seemed to forget that she wasn't real—not as she once had been. With tenderness, he helped her onto the seat next to him, and he nearly collapsed into her. He held her head carefully between his hands, his eyes brimming with unshed tears. She saw the war waging behind his eyes, the wonder, hope, and denial.

Hastily, he leaned in toward her for a kiss. It was rushed and desperate, and Annaleigh could do nothing but focus on staying solid for him, on staying real enough to give him one last kiss. It killed her all over again.

He came back to his senses quickly—too soon, she thought again; everything was happening too soon—and put space between them. He moved to the bench across from her again and looked down at his hands, at his fingers that had just woven through her hair.

"William…" Annaleigh said. She wanted to apologize. Not for the kiss, not for the flush she could see spreading across his face. She wanted to do anything to take away the pain she'd rekindled just by being by him. Just by remaining. But she bit her sorries. They would mean nothing to him. "I didn't mean to follow you. I… I was pulled here."

William found the locket again. He flipped it open and closed, staring out the window. He was allowed short flashes of relief when he didn't see her, when he could pretend the morning hadn't happened, that he hadn't seen her body by the lake and they had left, just as Mary had promised they would.

"I was thinking about you," he said.

I was thinking about you, too, she wanted to respond. *I will always be thinking about you.*

He opened his mouth as if to say something but only closed it, tensing his jaw and shaking his head.

"I'll be quiet," Annaleigh said. She let go of her focus, let herself fade from his world until she looked like the apparition she was. She wished she could make herself disappear entirely, but try as she could, she stayed visible. "Pretend I'm not here."

"I don't want to," he said, looking up at her. His eyes widened when he noticed the grayness she was shrouded in. He reached toward her, to touch her hand, but his fingers passed through her. She was mist; she was fog; she was gone but still there. "I don't want you do be gone. I want... I want to go back. To *save* you, to go with you. I want to go back to that lake and join you in its depths—"

"No. Do not be so selfish with your life." Her figure flashed back into focus before fading again.

"Selfish." He laughed and it was a terrible, desperate sound. "What is left for me?" His voice was raw, his heart bleeding out through his words. "There is no favor for me when I have lost everything. I should have known. I should have realized, and I should never have surfaced without you."

She shook her head, but he kept speaking.

"Either both of us should have survived or neither. This is not fair. This is *fate* being selfish."

"William." She remembered the way he'd fought back to the surface of the water, the relief she'd seen on the shore. "You fought for your life—for both of our lives. Don't stop fighting now."

"Why?"

She stared at him, made sure he met her eyes. "Mary."

It only took one name to break his resolve for self-destruction. She wasn't sure how long it would last, but it saved

143

him from the immediate danger of himself, and that was all she could do for the time being.

CHAPTER 19

The Cabin

MIDNIGHT HAD SWALLOWED THE LIGHT of the stars by the time William and Annaleigh arrived. The carriage jolted to a stop in front of a modest cabin built with logs and stone and fashioned to look as though it had been designed by the mountains themselves.

The cabin sat at nearly the highest peak of the range, perched on the edge of a cliffside, hugged by the forest on one side, and exposed to the sheer drop and expansive plains below. It was entirely alone on this desolate side of the mountain, too far from any sort of established town to see anything other than the occasional wilderness explorer.

It was the perfect place for contemplation and secrets. It was the perfect place for William, in this moment, to say goodbye to his wife, his Annaleigh.

William jumped out of the carriage, his bag over his shoulder. He paused briefly to offer his hand to help Annaleigh out of the carriage, but when he turned, she was already standing next to him. Her silent presence unnerved him, and though he wanted nothing more than to reach out and hold her hand, to touch her—to *really* touch her—he made his hand into a fist and buried it in his pocket.

The carriage left with its driver as he shoved open the stubborn front door of the cabin. All of the furniture inside was covered in large, white sheets, looking like hulking ghosts. It was an eerie sight, a pervasive stillness left over from the last tenants—his father and his grief.

"It's better than I imagined," Annaleigh said. She kept her voice low, worried that she would break the peacefulness of the cabin.

Everything was fragile and precarious. She felt that, if she were to step too heavily by the windows that overlooked the valleys below, the house would tip off the mountain, just as William would capsize if she spoke too much or too little. She was a ballerina on a tightrope that was miles above a circus she had no training to star in.

Without a word, William set his bags on the one bed off the small kitchen. He threw the meager belongings he'd brought into drawers and on top of dressers, looking over his shoulder every so often to find Annaleigh watching him from the doorway.

"You're scaring me," he said as he shoved the bag under the bed. "Standing there in the doorway like some—" *Ghost.*

He didn't say it out loud, but she heard it. She was his haunt, and there was nothing she could do to give him peace. His thoughts dragged her with him like she was tethered to his heart.

Annaleigh bit her lip and stepped away from the bedroom to explore the other parts of the cabin, trying to give him a wide berth as he settled in for the night. She could hear the conversation he was having with himself while she flipped on the lights in the library. He was arguing with himself, and it broke her heart. She could make out the way he scolded himself for snapping at her, for how badly he wanted to believe she wasn't gone—because it was impossible that she would still be there, that he could still see her.

Then she heard the locket snap open and closed, the creak of the bed as he sat down on it, and the exhale of breath as he finally let himself collapse in grief.

She sat in the far corner of the library on the floor, knees folded into herself as she pressed her spine against the leather-bound books behind her, and listened to him mourn her. Tears slid down her own face, much less fierce and ragged than his. She was silent as she squeezed her eyes closed, tore a hole in her cheek with her teeth, and listened.

The anguish of grief, it turned out, did not lessen once acknowledged. It wasn't as easy as a scraped knee, where a good cry would distract from the pain until the weeping stopped and the cut was bandaged. Once you touched it, grief only grew. It took on more, swallowed you whole until that's all there was. Grief was an egotistical emotion, unsatisfied until it became the only thing a person knew, the only thing they could see.

Annaleigh heard grief devour William until unconsciousness snatched away his tattered breaths. When she heard—*felt*—the stillness from the other room, she knew that it was safe for her to move again. To unfold herself from the floor, cross the small cabin, and watch him sleep from the doorframe.

The pillows were stained wet and he was dressed in the clothes he had been wearing that morning. Even his muddy shoes were still on, double knotted and hanging off the bed. She wanted to take them off, but she stopped herself. She didn't want to wake him, but even more so, she didn't want to try to untie them and have her fingers slip right through the laces.

So she settled on watching him, on focusing on the blotchy patches crying had stained on his cheeks, the smoothness of his brow in sleep. When she had centered herself enough that she felt confident in her substantiality, she found a blanket and placed it over him. He shifted, his arm reaching across the bed, searching for her. Instead, his fingers found nothing, and they tangled in the sheets under him.

Biting back a sob, she left the room, closed the door, and went to the windows. She stood and watched as the deep midnight sky became runny with the rising sun. She was so incredibly still, a stark contrast to the frantic pace of her thoughts.

Below, a farmer looked up to the cabin and thought he'd seen the sun glint off the pearly figure of a wispy girl. Then the light passed through her and she disappeared with the blink of an eye, but the inexplicable feeling of cold sadness stayed with him long into the warmth of the afternoon.

CHAPTER 20

The Nights

TIME PASSED STRANGELY FOR ANNALEIGH. What felt like a day was actually a week, and what she thought was only an hour of her time was a handful of afternoons for William. She didn't notice the discrepancy in its passage at first, but eventually, she felt the sluggish pull of her existence.

There was an unexpected exhaustion to her existence. She didn't sleep—couldn't sleep. She didn't feel as though she would even be able to if she'd attempted to. In all honesty, she was afraid of the night, worried that, if she closed her eyes for too long, she would never open them again. So instead, she spent hours in the dark remembering her brief life and fretting over the preservation of William's.

William had better days, days where he seemed to forget the horrid morning on the lakeshore. Every so often, a smile would accidentally spill across his face. He wasn't aware of the lightness that touched his eyes every now and then, but it brought a sense of peace and solace to Annaleigh. She became more confident that he could recover from everything that had happened when he smiled or laughed, and it pleased her even more to see that it sometimes even appeared to be genuine.

The good days, though, were underscored by terrible days. Days where he would not get out of bed. Days where he did nothing but stare at the wall and shrink away from her voice, from her touch. But the longer they stayed in the mountains, alone and isolated from the truth of it all, the fewer these days became.

Nearly every night, he managed sleep, though he would wake screaming, cold, and clammy from reliving the scene at the lake.

Some nights, he remembered saving her, dragging her stubbornly back to the surface, holding her on the shore, and begging her to come back to him. Other nights, he relived the wails of her father, of her mother, of himself as he knelt next to the body and soul of her. He would imagine the ghost of Annaleigh lying down, returning to the body he hadn't realized she'd been without.

The worst of the nightmares, though, involved him losing her, waking up to an empty cabin and a desolate mountain where no one cared what he'd lost, if he was lost.

Annaleigh tried to take William's mind off the nightmares. She distracted him with books from the library, with songs sung and stories of better times—of when they were children discovering love.

William managed his days and survived his nights. Mostly, he did so by lying to himself. It was the easiest thing to do. To live away from everyone in a cabin with the ghost of his love. He would stay there forever, isolated with his fictional life. There was no one to tell him she wasn't real, no one to walk right through her or look past her as though she were nothing more than floating dust motes.

The lie sustained him through the hard days and buoyed him up on the better ones, and he could go on pretending. Annaleigh let him. She didn't know what else to do, how else to save him. When the truth was unbearable, the lies he crafted for himself eased his pain, and she would have allowed anything in order to ease his pain.

Dozens of times, the façade broke. Annaleigh would fade to a gray figure and William would remember. He would trace her silhouette with his eyes—afraid his fingers would disappear her like smoke—and notice the hazy glint of something otherworldly. She was stitched into his world by the thinnest thread, and he wondered when it would snap, when she would become too great, too tired, too *incredible* to stay with him any longer.

William pretended not to notice when she drifted away, faded just enough for his heart to seize in his chest. He didn't want to dwell on it, to wonder what it meant that it was happening more and more. If he could live in the lie, if he could *believe* it enough, surely she could stay. His life didn't have to be so different; she wouldn't have to leave.

But then her hand would slip through his or he would reach out to brush her hair and stop himself, and the lie ate away at his heart until there was nothing but the truth left. The impossible, excruciating truth of it all. Annaleigh saw that the lie wouldn't hold for much longer.

William stayed up later and later every night talking to Annaleigh. Sleep was exchanged for stories of her—every story he hadn't already heard and some he already had. He wanted to know it all, to memorize the book of her life and to fill in the blank chapters he had been missing. He wondered why he hadn't asked her about her sisters when they were younger.

"They were so excited to get married," Annaleigh told him. She smiled for him, but her eyes were distant, in some other time. "Claire wanted to have a large family. Even when we were young and played house, she would have us all be her children. There was nothing she wanted more in life than to be a mother and a wife. Once, she told us she wanted a family of ten. My mother nearly fainted with joy. Ten! Can you even imagine?"

William laughed, looked at his hands. "I can."

But he wasn't imagining Claire and her husband with eight rowdy children running around their feet. He was imagining the children he was supposed to have with Annaleigh. He had had a dream of the daughter he might have had. They'd named her Sara after his mother, and in his dream, his daughter—with her rosy cheeks and bright blue eyes—had the stubbornness of her mother, the temper of her father, and Mary's propensity for French curses. She was perfect. She was impossible.

"I was afraid of becoming a mother," Annaleigh went on. Her eyes found his, and in the gray, she saw the sadness of possibilities, a deep ocean of *perhaps* and *never*. "I guess I don't have to be afraid of that anymore."

William turned away from her, changed the subject to something easier to hear, something lighter and sillier. "Do you recall the time we convinced Mary she was the child of a faerie and that I had found her in the woods as a boy?"

Annaleigh paused and studied the line of his back as he looked out the window. Some conversations were too real for him to consider. It heaped a heaviness onto his shoulders that he wasn't ready to carry yet. But she was concerned that the longer he ignored the truth, the harder it would be to accept when the time finally came. She didn't push him that night though. She laughed, humored him, and let the real world disappear for a little longer.

"I remember *you* telling her that lie," she said. "Oh how disappointed she was every evening when she returned from the woods without her faerie family."

Everything not spoken of, the stories left untold and ignored, darkened the corners of the cabins with shadows, and they were creeping closer.

CHAPTER 21

The Letter

THE STORIES WENT ON FOR days, and it had become almost easy to pretend that nothing had changed between them. *Almost* easy. There were still too many times he wanted to touch her, to brush his fingers along the curve of her neck and lean in to let his lips follow the path of his fingers. He always stopped himself, though, never let his wish turn to reality that would only wither and wilt in his mouth when he felt the truth of her body —the flimsy existence she maintained.

She never joined him in bed for the short hours he did sleep, and she was too quiet and still. For hours, she would stand perfectly motionless by the window, watching the world turn without her. It was unnatural, but William ignored the shivers of strangeness in favor for the possibility that she could stay with him forever.

That's all he asked for, all he prayed for whenever he saw her. He didn't ask for a way to travel back in time, for her to return to him as she once had been. He didn't beg the universe to make her real enough for him to touch, for a future to be truly possible for them as husband and wife. He simply wanted her to stay. That would be enough, because it had to be. It was easier than the other possibility: that she was gone until he joined her in whatever followed after life.

If anything followed at all. He didn't allow for that thought to last long enough to sink into his consciousness. He couldn't consider that there was nothing beyond living now, that he would *never* be allowed a life with Annaleigh. That thought would ruin him entirely. That thought would take away the last of his pathetic hope.

Mary still hadn't arrived, but she had sent a letter letting him know that she was taking care of things at home and would join him at her earliest convenience.

Will,

*The weather **has gotten much worse**. If the clouds' **temperament won't brighten** soon, **I fear it never will** stop raining! I'm sure the sun will shine again soon, and when it does, I'll be joining you. I'm leaving Samuel to tend after the house, and **I've seen** that the girls have time off. The house won't be in **terrible** conditions without them, and my **things** have been packed. **I'm worried** what Samuel will do in this large house **alone**. Perhaps he'll throw a party of his own. How **I hope I arrive** home early and catch him sliding down the banister with a bottle of champagne **in** his hand! What a hard **time** he'd have living that down. I bet he'd have **lies** ready to explain it away though. He's **never** caught improper. I wonder what the **help** does without us though. What do you think?*

*I'll see you soon, brother. If only this blasted rain would **stop**!*

*With love, **your Mary.***

Reading her letter, William could spot the care she had taken with choosing her words. She was being careful with him, and she'd made no mention of Annaleigh or their mother.

Annaleigh read the letter from over William's shoulder, and she noticed something odd, but she didn't mention it. When William went into the library for the afternoon to get lost in another world where the problems weren't his own, she reread the letter, circling certain words with her finger. There was a pattern to the note. Some words were darker, as if the pen had been dipped in more ink. It was a message for her, she realized. A message William wasn't supposed to notice.

Will has gotten much worse, temperament won't brighten. I fear it never will. I've seen terrible things. I'm worried, alone. I hope I arrive in time. Lies never help. Stop. With love, your Mary.

Annaleigh reread the message again and again. Mary had seen something. She said that William had gotten worse—but he seemed to be doing so much better. Annaleigh looked over her shoulder to the library. She noticed the way his face hung and his shoulders dropped when he thought she wasn't watching him. The shadows under his eyes had darkened so greatly that they looked like purple bruises. Was she helping him at all? Or making things worse, as she'd feared she would?

Lies never help. Stop.

She traced the word *stop*, noticed the jagged, shaky lettering. Mary was afraid, and Annaleigh should listen.

The lies William had mended himself with weren't helping. Perhaps in the short term, but the longer he believed them, the longer she let him hold the lies in his hands as truth, the worse he would be the day they were taken away from him. She had let his pretending go on for too long. Now, she had to hurt him all over again. She needed to rip out his poorly placed stitches, let him bleed again, and patch him properly. It would hurt, and his pain would be on her conscience, but Annaleigh had to be strong enough to do this for him.

She was the only one who could shake him from his stupor. She had to remind him of the world he lived in, the *real* world that existed outside of the cabin.

CHAPTER 22

The Truth

LATER THAT NIGHT, ANNALEIGH AND William fought.

Annaleigh hadn't meant to start a fight. She'd known that what she was going to say would be difficult to hear, to relive—for both of them—but it was a necessary pain. The burn of popping a shoulder back into its socket, the pinch of leeches extracting poisonous blood. The pain was unpleasant but temporary. She hoped.

Mary's letter had made it clear what she had to do: stop the lies. She couldn't let William go on pretending that everything was fine, that she was real and he could continue living with her as though nothing terrible had ever happened. But something terrible had happened. Telling himself otherwise didn't make it not true; it just delayed the inevitable.

Annaleigh wouldn't be able to go on living forever. She was tired—so tired—of focusing her energy. It was draining to live every day, every moment, in concentration, and she wasn't sure how long she'd be able to maintain it. When her energy would fade, so would she. For now, she'd only grown hazy, a gloomy figment in a vivid world. What if, one day, her energy sapped entirely and she vanished completely?

She couldn't go on telling stories of her former life as he fiddled with the locket, never reminiscing in his own stories. She couldn't let him ignore the fire that was burning around him simply because he didn't want to put it out. She had to remind him, to make it clear that she didn't belong here anymore. She didn't belong to him anymore.

Annaleigh belonged somewhere else—somewhere mysterious and unexplored to her, but somewhere she wanted to see. There had to be something to greet her when she finally stopped existing, because this life was done with her.

It was a hard thing for her to admit. She preferred the lie, just as William did. Admitting to herself that what had happened was real frightened her, and when she was scared, there was nothing she was better at than denial. But she had to move past it, to embrace everything that had happened and would happen, for William.

She needed to take the locket from him, but he never let it out of his sight. He had placed all of his hope in the locket, and she suspected he kept the truth locked within it, too. If she could open it, let it all spill out...

The other night, she had watched William sleep and seen how he clung to the locket. He hadn't set it down once, not even to bathe. She imagined him accidentally dropping it off the side of the mountain when he went out for a walk, pictured how she would waft away on the wind as it fell, lost to him for good. Half of her wanted him to lose it on his own, to have it be an accident that took her away from him. Annaleigh didn't want to have to do it herself. She wasn't sure she would be strong enough.

The thought of him losing her like that, though, broke her in half. It snapped her from the fairytale she'd allowed William to live in for the past weeks. It couldn't come to that. He couldn't lose her because of an accident, not again, and Annaleigh could no longer go on living in his lies. It was starting to wear on her, the fiction hanging on her uncomfortably like bristly fabric.

William came out of the library to settle on the couch in front of the window, and he motioned for Annaleigh to join him. It was their ritual every night, to sit in front of the stars and remember, for him to ask questions about the years he hadn't known her and for her to indulge him with stories. But tonight, when she saw him sitting there with a shadow of a smile, Mary's words urged Annaleigh to tell a different story, a story that would hit him with a truth as painful as a punch. The lies, she realized now, did more harm than good—for both of them.

Lies never help. Stop.

So that night, when Annaleigh settled next to William and he asked her for a story, she told him the one he had never wanted to hear.

"Well, you know how anxious I get in crowds," she began. "There was this one night when my corset was so restrictive that I was sure my lungs were punctured by bones—only I wasn't sure if the bones were that of my ribs or the corset."

He laughed and picked up her hand, stopping her fingers from picking at the frayed edge of the couch. He didn't let his hand linger on hers. He never did anymore, and it made her ache, but she pressed on.

"So I asked to get some air. Asked isn't the right word, really... Demanded may be more accurate. I was surprised you heard me. My breath felt so shallow that I wasn't sure I would be able to speak anything above a whisper, but somehow you heard, even over the celebration. As I was going outside, you were stopped by this man. I can't remember who, but I remember that he wouldn't stop chatting you up, so you told me to go ahead without you and you would meet me."

William stiffened. She could hear his breathing come faster, see his eyes losing their focus on her.

"I ran down to the lake to wait. I remember thinking how otherworldly it all looked. The bones of our wedding — the chairs, the arch... It was beautiful and supernatural, and I could have sworn I saw Sara sitting in one of the chairs. Maybe I did. Maybe I didn't imagine that."

"Stop," William said.

Annaleigh didn't, couldn't.

"I could breathe easier out of the house, away from the crowds. But I still needed to cool down, so I walked across the dock and dipped my fingers into the water. When I stood, there was this great bird, darker than even the shadows in the woods. It swooped down at me, grabbing for my locket, and I tripped backward over myself and went sprawling across those soggy boards. Before I could even catch the breath that had been knocked out of me, I heard the skitter and plunk of the locket falling into the water..." She reached out with her free hand and ran her fingers over the brass locket around William's neck. "I had to get it back."

"Annaleigh, stop," he begged. It was a weak plea, and though she had heard it, she knew she had to keep going. He couldn't live in the lie anymore.

"My wedding dress was already ruined at this point, so I didn't see the harm in crawling across the dock. I grabbed after the locket, but I kept missing. I nearly lost it so many times. I just kept thinking how disappointed you and Mary would be, how heartbroken I would be to lose something so precious, and then I caught it just with the hook of my fingers. I pulled it out and hooked it on the last post of the dock. That's where you found it, isn't it?"

"*Please.*"

"My heart surged when I saved it, but I had leaned over too far. I lost my balance and tipped forward, off the dock, and into the water. You know, when I put my hand in the lake earlier, I didn't think it was that cold, but when I plunged into that black water, I knew I was wrong. It was freezing—as cold as winter itself—and it burrowed into my bones."

He started trembling, and she lowered her hand from the necklace to place on top of his. He fidgeted beneath her touch, but he didn't move away from her. Not yet.

"You know the one thing you should never do when you fall into freezing-cold water? Open your mouth."

He looked away from her, his eyes searching for something else to focus on. Anything to make this stop. Anything to ignore the truth.

"That was my first mistake," Annaleigh continued. "I keep thinking about how *stupid* it had been. I knew better than that. I had fallen in cold water before. You pushed me in when we were kids one year, right at the end of fall. I didn't open my mouth then, but that night, for some reason, I did. It's like all of my senses went rushing out of my head as the water filled me up."

William tried to pull away from her, but she focused her strength on keeping him still, on keeping him listening.

"My wedding dress was so heavy. I never would have thought it would be that heavy, but the water… It just was too much." She searched his face and saw the dread grow, the sick look he got in his eyes as he imagined it, pictured her fighting the pull of her wedding dress. She knew he was seeing her on the shore, covered in a white sheet, and caught in the great skirts of her dress, looking smaller than she ever had.

"I fought so incredibly hard, William. Please know that. I didn't give up, even as my muscles burned and my lungs cried for oxygen. I didn't stop fighting. I wanted to. It would have been easier, but I fought. For you, for Mary, for myself. It wasn't enough," Annaleigh said. "The dress was my anchor, and it pulled me down too fast. I tangled in it, and I remember thinking how simple it would be to just sleep down there forever."

The stars outside the window seemed to dim.

"I touched the bottom, William."

He made a noise in the back of his throat, something that sounded like a broken sob. Annaleigh saw him work the muscles of his jaw as he chewed up a scream.

"We had never made it to the bottom of the lake before, but I did," she said, softer this time. "It's even deeper than we thought, did you know that? And then I saw Sara, just as you broke through the surface of the water."

CHAPTER 23

The Break

THIS TIME, WHEN WILLIAM TRIED to take his hand from hers, he managed. He jumped from the couch and crossed the room in several large, angry strides. He kept his back to Annaleigh, ran his shaking fingers through his tangled hair. She could see his shoulders rising and falling too quickly.

"It didn't hurt," Annaleigh lied to him. It was a small allowance she gave the story.

It was bad enough that he had to live with knowing he was too late—she knew how much he blamed himself for it. It was worse that he had seen her after the fact, her pallor waxy and blue, her lips cold and dark. She didn't need him to know how panic-stricken her final moments had been. She didn't want him to know that she had never felt a pain so enormous in all her life. She didn't even want Mary to know that.

"It happened fast," she said. "So fast."

William turned on her then, eyes furious.

"I told you to *stop. STOP.* I don't want to hear it. I don't want to think—" His fingers found his hair again. He didn't seem to know how to hold himself, how to keep all the emotions that raged within him contained. So he exploded. "*You never should have been there.*"

"What?"

"I put you there. I put you in danger, and I was too late!"

Annaleigh stood from the couch and the moonlight seeped through her. The vision of her there, glowing and so extraordinarily unnatural, set him spiraling further. He couldn't cope with losing his illusions. Now he felt like he was the one drowning.

"How is this fair?" he yelled. "How is it fair that you are here but *not* here? That I am to see you every day, every moment of my waking life—which is most now, for I cannot sleep without nightmares of you—but I cannot do anything? That you are so near yet so far away. I cannot touch you. I cannot kiss you or hold you…"

"William," she said, stepping from the moonlight, closer to him.

"*No!*" His voice was harsh, destroyed. He ran his hands over his face, turned away from her, and let his anger spill from him like poison. "I have no future with the dead. The lies are not enough." As he said it, he realized he meant it.

Living with the lies he told himself every morning and every night had sustained him, but he was still starving for truth. For something real and impossible. He was dying with her, without her. He would do anything to have her stay, to have her leave. To have her be real. And yet…

"*You* are not enough, Annaleigh. Not anymore."

Annaleigh took a step back. She could do nothing but watch as he fell apart, untangled the knots of his rage and grief, and let them collect on the ground around his feet only to be stomped on. She watched as he leaned over the table, arms spread wide and shoulders heaving.

"You are a curse to me, and I will never escape," he said, his words flat and hot. "I'm haunted by every mistake I've ever made, all incarnated in you."

"I'm...sorry," she said, and it was pitiful. It wasn't enough — sorries never were — but there was nothing she could say, no solace she could offer him.

"You're apologizing?" William laughed, and it was terrible. "What happened to sorries being meaningless when you can't do anything to change the circumstances, Annaleigh?"

"I have nothing else to give. Sorry is all I have," she said, quiet, hurt.

"I don't want it. It would have been easier to have never met you than feel this pain," he said. "It would have been easier for me to have drowned with you that night. It would be easier if I never saw you again."

He could draw blood with his pointed words, but Annaleigh knew he meant none of them. Not truly. It was the desperate anger of a hopeless man. Someone who had been beaten and bloody but managed to stand, shaky on his feet, with his fists still raised, ready to strike.

"I love you," Annaleigh said. "I cannot explain fate, and I have no reason for how or why our lives are this way."

"Our lives," he whispered, shaking his head.

Annaleigh was trembling; she was breaking. "There is no going back to fix the flaws in our destiny, William. Our time together has to be enough. It's all we have."

She could hear the snag of his breath, the furious beating of his stubborn heart, which he wanted nothing more than to silence.

"Our love," she said, whispered, "was too heavy to hold in one life. It goes on, even now. It will always exist, no matter how we exist, no matter when…"

His head dropped between his shoulders, a valley between two peaks. He thought of how she had walked into his life and filled him entirely. She had repaired every piece of him that had been empty for so long, fixing him in a way no one ever could, in a way he'd never known was possible. From the first moment he'd laid eyes on her, she'd been all he could dream of, and he had become all she would ever think of. With each passing moment, they shaped one another. They held fire in their fingerprints, a light that illuminated even the darkest parts of the other. Each touch he shared with her, she returned.

They were sacred. But in this world, in this now, they were broken.

"I will never be sorry for a moment, a breath, I spent with you. I wouldn't trade it for a thousand years of anything else," Annaleigh said, hushed. "We had a finite forever."

"It wasn't enough," he said.

"It has to be. William—" His name was a flower on her tongue, a carnation blooming in the light of love.

Suddenly, she was behind him, her cold fingers tracing the curve of his spine, counting his bones with her delicate touch, and he'd had all he could bear.

He picked up the glass in front of him and threw it at the door of the cabin. Its shattering punctuated his fury over fate. "It wasn't! It never will be!"

For William, grief was only two steps away from savagery. It was a terrible trait he'd inherited from his father, and he'd only seen flashes of it in him. The turbulence of pain could quickly turn outward, directed from within at whatever target stepped in front of it. That was what curled inside of William then, what found relief in the destruction he delivered to the cabin.

He found another glass and slammed it to the table, the shards cutting into his palm. With a bloody hand, he swiped the table clear of its contents, sent everything scattering to the floor.

He didn't care—he didn't care about anything anymore but fury. When he rounded on his mess, he found an empty room, trashed and overturned by his rage.

A spike of panic surged in his heart, and his wrath reeled back for a moment. He touched the locket on his neck, clutching at it desperately as he looked around for Annaleigh, confused, terrified.

"Annaleigh?" He searched the cabin, looking in the library, the bathroom, his bedroom... All empty. He opened the front door of the cabin and called out into the dark woods. "Annaleigh!"

She stood behind him, her hand resting on his shoulder as tears fell down her translucent cheeks. She saw them land on him and turn to nothing, the same nothing she was made of.

William turned back to the cabin, eyes wide and brimming. He looked through her, walked past her, and buckled to the floor.

CHAPTER 24

The Savior

THE CHAIN OF THE LOCKET snapped as William pulled it from his neck. He opened it, fidgeting with the latch as he called for Annaleigh again and again, his apologies dropping to the ground with his tears.

"Please," he said to no one, to everyone. "Please. I didn't mean it. I didn't mean what I said—every moment was worth it. You will always be enough!"

Annaleigh followed behind him as he searched for her, and try as she could to make herself visible to him again, she remained unseen, insubstantial.

"I didn't mean it," William repeated.

"I know," Annaleigh said, but her words fell on deaf ears. "I know. I hear you."

The sun rose on William as he continued searching for Annaleigh, unwilling to accept that she was truly gone to him. He stumbled out of the cabin and into the woods, thinking he'd seen a flash of fabric, the flutter of a dress disappearing behind trees, but he found nothing. The sun shone through the branches as he followed his delusions deeper into the woods. As it grew dark again, he fell to the ground, laid his head back on the trunk of a tree. Exhaustion pulled him under.

He awoke the next morning, very confused and very lost. Annaleigh waited behind him when he stood, put her hand on his back, and helped guide him back to the cabin, though he didn't feel the pressure of her fingers, didn't realize he would have been hopelessly lost without her.

Her absence screamed in the empty cabin, and he searched for her again, hoping beyond hope that she might have returned in the night. But the rooms were still empty, nothing disturbed from how he had left it. The cabin was still trashed from his outburst the other night, but he didn't have the mind to pick it up. He wouldn't pick it up until he found her.

So he searched again, called her name all day and all night. Huddled by the window, he whispered to the moon, pleading for her to come back to him. He wished with every ounce in him that this were another one of his nightmares, that he hadn't really lost her forever. He couldn't stand forever alone. He wouldn't survive it.

William's hope soured in his stomach and rolled violently in his head. He forgot to eat, forgot to bathe, forgot to sleep as he begged for her. She never left him though. Annaleigh stayed through it all, absorbing the force of his grief in her gut. She cried quietly next to him every night, overlooked and unseen.

His quiet begging rose to shouts when he found the liquor in the kitchen cabinet. Bottles emptied and stacked around him, cluttered on the ground. They clinked together when he stood and went to the window, calling out to the stars at night and the fog of the morning. He implored her return, demanded justice from fate, but he was ignored.

Nothing changed, and he remained alone.

His frantic searching slowed as his hope dwindled away, and then it stopped entirely when he could no longer move. He sat, catatonic, in front of a pathetic fire as the woods tapped at his front door in the dead of night. With vacant eyes, he looked out the front windows, and when he swore he saw a figure, he ran to answer the rapping. The door swung wide, opening to emptiness.

The wind, his mind explained for him as his face fell. He closed the door and secured it tight, but the knocking at his door did not quiet. It went on through the night—a scratching, rapping sound, persistent and unnerving. Madness crept close to him, reaching with lonely arms for an embrace. William reached out to meet it.

Annaleigh was helpless. She ached to comfort him, to steal his pain away and accept it as his own. But nothing she did made any difference. He never heard her, no matter how loudly she screamed that she was still there with him. He couldn't feel her when she stroked his cheek, his hair, when she hugged him or laid gentle kisses across his brow. She was useless, a bystander as he fell into oblivion.

She cared for him covertly, pulling thick blankets to his shoulders when he fell asleep with liquor in his hands. She extinguished the candles that burned dangerously low before they had a chance to light the cabin ablaze. She sang to him, and while she was sure he couldn't hear her, there were times she thought he felt her presence.

Another week spilled away. The collection of bottles around the couch grew.

William never went back to the bedroom. He stole moments of sleep on the couch, unwilling to leave the last place he had seen Annaleigh on the off chance she would return.

Before he knew it, Mary arrived. She had to nearly kick in the front door when William wouldn't answer her knocking — since he thought it was the mysterious rapping taunting him again—but Annaleigh had found a way to turn the lock. Mary stumbled inside, took a look at her then William, and immediately sprang into action.

She didn't ask for an explanation of what had happened, didn't need a reason. She saw her brother, how far gone he appeared, how quiet and thin he had become, and knew she had made it just in time. She hadn't been too late.

Mary washed him, shaved his face, which had grown dusty with scruff. With conviction and a string of curses, she forced soup past his lips and poured the last of his whisky down the sink.

It didn't take long for her to realize that William couldn't see Annaleigh, that the locket was useless to him now, though he refused to let it go. Its power had drained, and Annaleigh's tether to this Earth was pulling thin.

Days passed in silence as she slowly bandaged her broken brother. She pulled books from the library to read to him, but William never looked at her, never acknowledged that she was even there. He only continued to stare—out the window, at the wall, at his hands, at the faulty locket.

One day, Annaleigh spoke to Mary as she wrapped her brother in a blanket on the couch he refused to leave. She had been careful not to say too much since she had arrived, worried it would be hard on Mary to help her brother when she was still being haunted herself. Annaleigh didn't want to get in the way, didn't want to be more of a burden than she had already been.

"I don't know what happened," she told Mary. "He was screaming, and he said it would be easier for him to never see me again. And then, he didn't."

Mary nodded but didn't say anything in response. William was distant but still awake—his eyes open but unfocused. She wasn't sure if he would notice her answering no one. She thought better than to risk it.

"I've watched him every night. I made sure…" Annaleigh shook her head, wrung her hands. "I tried to make sure nothing happened. If you hadn't arrived when you did… I don't know if I could have stopped him."

Sighing, Mary ran her hand over her brother's forehead, pushing back his damp hair. "I'm sorry," she said to both William and Annaleigh. "I'm here now. I won't let anything happen."

"I didn't mean to hurt him," Annaleigh said. "I can't be here and hurt him, but I can't leave. I'm stuck."

"I'm going to take a walk," Mary said to William. "I will be right back."

Grabbing her cloak from a hook by the front door, Mary went outside, Annaleigh next to her.

"Does he know I'm still here?" Annaleigh asked.

Mary walked a bit farther, looked back at the cabin, and shook her head. "I can't tell. He does not see you, but that doesn't mean he can't feel you. Your presence is very strong. Sometimes I can still smell your perfume."

"Then he must be able to, too."

"He might. He won't let me take the locket," she said. "He thinks that you might come back."

"Can I?"

"Would you?" Mary asked, looking up at her. She took a seat on a fallen tree, and Annaleigh joined her. They glanced back at the cabin and watched the curling smoke of the chimney join the clouds above. "Would that be the best thing to do after all of this?"

Annaleigh hesitated. "I… I am not sure. I want to help, but I'm not sure if I can. Where is your mother?"

Mary chewed her bottom lip before answering. "Home. She's bound there. Her tether is the house, as yours is Will."

"I would have thought her tether would be you and William, her children."

"We are, just…not as we are now. Our residual energies, as children, haunt the house. Sara stays there, looks after us. She watches us grow up. She was never able to do that while she was alive. Father took her away, kept her for himself. I don't think she wants to leave. I'm not sure she can."

"Oh," Annaleigh said.

She bit her lip, chewing on her thoughts. She pictured William as a child, remembering how loud and defiant he had been. The image was irreconcilable to the man he now was—an empty husk of his former self. But he wasn't as bad as he had been. She didn't need to watch him every second anymore, afraid of what he would do to himself. His eyes were still vacant, and he was too quiet, but he had more color. He looked more alive than he had before. Mary, though, had paled of her color.

"You're helping him, Mary," Annaleigh said.

Mary laughed. It was a bleak, miserable sound swallowed by the woods at their back. "Am I?"

"You didn't see him before. It was…much worse." So much worse, though Annaleigh was too afraid to tell Mary exactly how bad he'd become.

He hallucinated shadows, shadows that he wanted to be hers but never were. He only had nightmares—at all hours of the day, any time when he was too tired to keep staring at the nothing around him. He always woke screaming, shaking, and often he got sick. She could only imagine what he saw, what made him run to the toilet and purge his already empty stomach.

And the knocking on the front door—she was sure he would lose what little of his sanity was left if he kept hearing the rapping. She didn't know where the sound came from, but it made her nerves sear and her head spin every time she heard it. Once, he'd opened it, toting the gun he had taken down from above the fireplace. He was met by a black raven with glassy eyes. It cawed at him, raw and horrible, and the sound tore through the silent cabin. William shot at it until it flew away. Annaleigh was glad he had used up the bullets on something other than himself.

"There's only so much I can do," Mary said, staring at her hands in defeat. "If he gives up, it doesn't matter how much soup I force-feed him. He has to want to live, too. I can't do all the work."

They stayed together, sat on the rough log as the sun set and night swam across the sky.

Part 5

But our love it was stronger by far than the love
Of those who were older than we —
Of many far wiser than we —
And neither the angels in Heaven above
Nor the demons down under the sea
Can ever dissever my soul from the soul
Of the beautiful Annabel Lee;

— Stanza V, *Annabel Lee* by Edgar Allan Poe

CHAPTER 25

A Conversation

WHEN MARY WENT BACK INSIDE, William was waiting for her at the front door. He had a blanket around his shoulders and his feet were bare, but his eyes were clearer than they'd been in weeks. He carried accusations in his pockets, held a feeling of betrayal behind his back like a secret he could barely keep hidden.

"Who were you talking to?" he asked. His words were harsh, whittled away by a dagger of distrust.

"Look who's up and speaking again," Mary said. She turned from him to close and lock the door, being careful to avoid reaching through Annaleigh without making it obvious that she wasn't alone.

"That's not an answer to my question," he said, his eyes narrowing.

"No one, Will." Mary hung up her cloak and looked over him, noticing the chain knotted around his fist. "Can I have that?" she asked, nodding to the locket.

He looked down, staring at the locket as if he hadn't realized he was still holding it. "No," he said. "She might come back. She's going to come back."

Mary stepped up to him and wrapped her hand around his. "She's not coming back, Will." She tried to take the locket from his grasp, but he only tightened his fist around it as he pulled away.

"Who were you talking to outside?" he asked again. His stare became sharper as he studied her face. "I heard you talking to someone. It was her, wasn't it?"

Annaleigh watched as Mary fought for an excuse. She could have told him that he'd imagined it—it wasn't a stretch to say that he was hearing and seeing things that weren't there. He might have believed her, too, but she would never hand him that lie. She could have told him that she'd been talking to herself, but he'd see right through that.

When she couldn't find an excuse, an explanation she was satisfied with, Mary just moved away, going into the kitchen to busy herself with making supper.

"It was her," William repeated, following Mary. His eyes were bloodshot and his hair stood up in strange tufts, worked into knots by his anxious fingers. There was a sense of urgency in his posture, a vibration coming from him that made Mary nervous.

Annaleigh walked just behind him, running her hand over his arm as she passed, and he settled slightly.

"Don't lie to me, Mary. I've had enough of lies," he said. "You've told me nothing for years—about what you see, what you hear. I know you still see her. I *know* it."

"Will…"

"I can see it in your eyes," he accused. "Don't think I don't notice how they focus on nothing but air. You saw her at the shore. Even when I threw the locket away, you still saw her, and you still see her now, don't you? Tell me you still see her." He spoke quickly, desperately.

Mary took a deep breath.

"Please." His plea tore across his rough voice. "Tell me you see her."

"Will, it was nothing," she said. The pan clattered in the sink. "I hope you like soup, because it's the only thing I know how to really prepare. Though I'm growing tired of it already."

"How can you still see her?" he pressed. "I have the locket, and I cannot... Why you? What right have you to see her, when she was—is—my wife?"

"Stop it, Will. Stop!" Mary turned to him and let the vegetables she had been cutting roll across the counter. "Don't you see what you're doing to yourself? She's gone."

William flinched at her voice, at the tone she'd spoken to him with. He had been living in the fog of silence for too long, and he had forgotten the vigor of Mary. It was like ice water being splashed across his face.

"She's not."

"She is. And even if she weren't, do you really still want to see her after everything that's happened? You can't get her back."

"I could talk to her. I could *see* her, be with her. That would be enough!" William paced the floorboards, his fingers working knots into his hair. "That would be enough," he said softly, to himself.

Mary looked up at him, met his gaze, and held it fiercely with her own. "You don't know what it's like, Will. You don't know the toll it takes."

Annaleigh hovered behind Mary. "*Mary*," she sighed.

"I loved her, too, you know," Mary said, a tear falling down her face. She swiped at it angrily and went back to cutting up the vegetables. "It's selfish for you to be the only one allowed to grieve."

"You can grieve—"

"No, I can't," she said. Annaleigh stepped next to Mary and laid a kiss on her cheek, a gentle apology with the press of her lips. "I can't grieve Anna when I'm worried about you killing yourself. I don't have the luxury to say goodbye to my best friend—my sister—when I'm worried my brother could be next. I don't have time to focus on myself when I need to focus on you. On *saving you*."

William took a step back and slumped into a chair. He looked at nothing, thinking about the pain he had hoarded for himself, the way he'd denied Mary the chance to feel anything because he felt too much. There was a selfish part of him that reared up, that said he deserved to keep the grief, that no one else could possibly feel as anguished as he.

Annaleigh had been *his* wife; she had been *his* best friend. She held his heart, his soul, and she'd left him alone. Mary didn't understand what it was like to have your heartbroken, torn out of your chest, but still feel it beating stupidly behind your ribs. She'd been never in love; she'd never lost her soulmate. She'd lost her mother. She couldn't comprehend what he was going through; she never would.

But, he realized, she didn't have to. She didn't have to match his memories, his feelings, to grieve. Pain hit people in different ways. Annaleigh's death was a ripple, washing out over every person who had ever been lucky enough to have had their life touched by her. You didn't have to know her well to feel the devastation of loss.

Mary had loved her. She loved her nearly as much as William did, and she'd been as alone as he had. They were both left in solitary with their separate grief. He didn't see why they couldn't feel it together, why they shouldn't share each other's strength when the other was weak and beaten down. She had lifted him up from as far as he'd fallen, but no one had given a hand to her.

William didn't see Annaleigh move next to him, didn't feel the whisper as she leaned in toward him and spoke in his ear, "Live for Mary." But he heard it. He heard her voice from another night.

He needed to fight; he needed Mary—he needed to keep fighting for Mary. He owed her that much.

"I'm a bastard," he said, refocusing his eyes on Mary. "I've been selfish. I'm always selfish. You love her too."

"I do," Mary said, chopping the last of the vegetables and sliding them into the pan. She lit a fire on the stove and began cooking the soup.

"She loved you too, Mary," William said.

Mary looked up and locked eyes with Annaleigh. "I know she did."

"I still do. More than almost everything," Annaleigh added, resting her hand over William's.

He looked up at her touch but didn't let the hope of her scorch through him like a hot poker. It was impossible; it was wishful thinking. She wasn't here. She was gone. Her presence— her touch—would have been too good, and he wasn't worthy of a kindness from the universe, not after how selfish he'd been. Annaleigh wasn't coming back.

"How long have you...seen things?" William asked, trying to change the subject to something less painful. It was odd to think that talking about his sister's supernatural abilities was considered easy conversation, but nowadays, it was a topic that touched the least amount of open wounds.

"I was seven. Remember when grandfather passed?" Mary asked, leaning back against the counter. "He came to me that night, stood right at the foot of my bed, and said goodbye to me.

He wanted me to tell Mother that he loved her and he would wait for her."

"And since then?"

"I see a lot. Specters mostly—those who have passed. Some people I know. Others I don't. There are those who ask for help and those who just want an explanation. Most don't understand what's happened to them. They don't know where to go, what to do. It's confusing right after they've died."

"What do they look like to you?"

"Like people. But *not*." She pursed her lips, thinking. "It's like an old photograph of a person, a little faded and fuzzy around the edges. They don't quite look right in their surroundings, like they were cut from their life and pasted into someone else's photo album. *My* photo album."

"Is it frightening?" William asked, putting his head down on the table and turning over the locket.

"It was when I was younger and didn't know what was happening. Mother explained it."

"Sara could see things?" Annaleigh asked.

"She could," Mary answered before she stopped herself. When William looked up at her, she amended her words. "She could see things, too, I mean. Our mother. It might have been because of the locket, maybe something in our blood, or a combination of both. I'm not sure. It was only scary when I thought of them as ghosts, though. As something from a horror story."

"Isn't that what they are?"

"You saw Annaleigh," Mary said quietly. She saw her name hit him, saw the slight flinch, the shaking it brought to his fingers. "Was she scary?"

He lowered his head again, rested his cheek on the rough wood of the table. "No."

"They're people...just different. No one ever truly leaves us."

"You should have told me earlier," William said. "I could have, I don't know, helped."

"I *did* tell you. About Mother. After she had died. I told you how our house was haunted, but you just laughed — which is fine. I would have laughed if things had been reversed. Besides, there was nothing you could do," Mary said, shrugging. "There's nothing *I* can do, really. I can talk to them, and that's it. I can't change the things I see in my dreams."

"What do you dream?"

"What *don't* I dream," Mary said with a dark laugh. "I see everything or nothing. It's either blackness or fates, things that will happen that I can't do a damn thing about. Remember the girl who was hit by the train in town?"

William nodded, his cheek scratching against splinters.

"I saw her die a month before she showed up in my room in the middle of the night. I didn't know when it would happen. I just knew that it would."

"And...Annaleigh?" He didn't want to ask, but he had to. He had to know, and he didn't want to know.

Mary watched him carefully, but he wouldn't meet her eye. He was intentionally looking everywhere but at her.

"Yes, I saw that too. At least a dozen times, I dreamt it, each in a slightly different way, so I wasn't sure which was real. I wasn't supposed to see it at all, I think. But I did. I wish I hadn't."

William sat up, nodded a few times, and stood. "I think I'm going to go to bed now," he said.

"What about dinner?" Mary asked, looking after him.

He stopped at the doorframe, just where Annaleigh had stood to watch him the first night they'd spent here. "I am growing quite tired of soup, now that you mention it." A light smile lifted his mouth, and it was just enough to tell Mary that she hadn't lost him entirely.

He could be saved.

"He will be saved," Annaleigh said, giving a voice to Mary's thoughts. "One day, he will be fine."

That night, after William had awoken from another nightmare and found Mary on the couch, he joined her. They held each other as they cried over Annaleigh. Mary clung to her older brother just as tightly as he clung to her. They were the stubborn, wispy seeds of a dandelion in a tumultuous storm, refusing to be blown away by the raging winds. They held tight, huddled close, trembling as they finally released the grief they'd been storing deep within themselves.

Mary and William cried over their mother, their father, their childhood that had slipped away too quickly, and then they returned to Annaleigh. They remembered her, every great and perfect thing she'd brought into their lives, and they cried until they were laughing, until their painful memories diluted into happier ones. William hugged his small sister close to him as they said their goodbyes to the world they'd known, the one that had held the girl with the angelic, blond hair and starlit spirit. They fell asleep under the moon and in front of the dying fire as they whispered farewell the girl they both loved most.

Annaleigh watched on and felt a new lightness. She could hear whispers beyond her world, beckoning her forth, but she wasn't ready yet. She still had to say her own goodbyes.

CHAPTER 26

A Reminder

MORE THAN ANYTHING, MARY'S PRESENCE—her chattering and bickering with herself, with the mess, with him—rebuilt William.

It was a slow and arduous recovery. For every three days that he smiled and spoke with bright eyes and a clear voice, there was one terrible day where everything seemed hopeless. Those days were as bad as before Mary.

William wouldn't get out of bed. He'd just lie there, staring at nothing. Sometimes he screamed, cried out, fought against the world and his life. Mary would hold him down, talk nonsense to try to calm him down.

Annaleigh would stand by, watching, wishing things were better. On bad days when he managed to heave himself out of bed, he would stagger outside and sit on the edge of the mountain to empty a bottle of liquor he had hidden away. Mary would find him that evening, coax him back inside with a warm blanket, and let him sleep on the couch. She kept him far away from any ledges he could fall off of, any ledges he could jump from.

The bleak days when the storm inside William brewed violently were horrible, but they were growing few and far between. The day after his backslides, he would wake up as if nothing had happened. Everything, it would seem, was fine. It was an odd scene, and the juxtaposition of his disposition, spaced only by a few hours, startled Annaleigh.

But Mary had seen it before. She knew that this was the way it was with William. Three steps forward, one stumble back. It had been like that with Sara, with George... The only difference now was that Mary was alone in putting him back together. Where once Annaleigh's laughter or voice had pieced him whole, Mary had to fill the silence.

Little by little, it was working. It just took longer than before for William to feel human again, for him to start accepting that life went on without Annaleigh. The sun still rose and set, the wind still breezed warm, and lightning bugs still lit the twilight skies like stars fallen to earth. And he would go on, too.

Mary asked again about the locket, imploring William to give it back to her.

"I'll keep it safe," she promised. "You know I will."

"Why can't I keep it?" he asked, pulling the locket away from her though she had yet to reach for it.

Mary frowned. "It's weighing you down."

"It's reminding me—"

"*Exactly*," Mary said. "That's the problem."

"It's the solution," William said, an excitement surging through his voice. "It's reminding me why I have to go on. It's reminding me of her, what she would think on those days when I'm so close to..." He shook his head, turned away from Mary before she noticed the dark cloud pass behind his eyes.

He'd only briefly considered ending his life, but he had shied away from the idea immediately. He believed he was a coward, but when Annaleigh saw the resolve drain from him to destroy himself, she had never thought him braver.

William didn't only fear being without Annaleigh, it seemed. He feared the pain death would bring, the uncertainty of what would come next. But more importantly, he feared the disappointment he'd see if he met Annaleigh in the next life. She'd never forgive him for wasting his life.

He could imagine the lecture she would give him. She thought he was more than he was—braver, stronger, *better*. Only when he gave up would he truly lose her forever. So he had to be better for her. He chose to be better.

William felt the locket under his thumb. "I need to keep it, Mary. For today, I need to keep it."

Mary watched him, noticed the glittering figure of Annaleigh beside him. She looked so much more peaceful, so much happier. When Annaleigh saw her staring, she smiled at her.

Annaleigh didn't have to say anything. Mary could see for herself that William had made it past the worst of it. The agony of his grief had dulled, and the memories of Annaleigh would no longer level him, but rather lift him up. She could see it in his posture, the straight line of his spine. Even the defiant tilt to his chin was back. William was coming back to Mary, returning to the real world.

"Love you, Will," Mary said.

"And you, Mary," he said, letting the locket lie back on his chest.

The days grew brighter; the nights seemed less dark and dreadful. William began sleeping more, and once she was sure her brother had started to find a slice of peace, Mary finally slept. No visions haunted her dreams, and no ghosts sought her out in the middle of the night. Only Annaleigh remained.

For every week that passed, it became easier for William to live—
to cope with the fact that the world spun on without Annaleigh.
He still woke with a burning hole in his chest, as if someone had
tamped out their cigar on his heart. There was never a day that
passed where he didn't think about Annaleigh, but his
nightmares of her slowly became dreams.

For a while, he thought of her nearly every second,
remembering the way she'd watched him do simple things, the
way her eyes would glint when they shared a silent joke. He
didn't know that she still sat next to him, watching him the same
way she always had.

Eventually, he thought of her less. William didn't imagine
what she would be doing if she were there with him every
moment. He thought of her every hour, and then just a few times
a day. When he realized she crossed his mind less frequently, he
surged with guilt and would commit the rest of his day to
remembering her, to picturing every small feature of her face and
every story she had told him over those nights they'd stayed up
until sunrise.

The guilt faded over time, and he was less attentive to
Mary's strange behavior. He didn't notice when she looked next
to him, at nothing—at Annaleigh—and smiled. He didn't hear
the conversations she had with Annaleigh—or if he did, he
didn't say anything.

Life didn't hurt him as much. It was a tolerable pain.

That, he realized, was what living without Annaleigh would
have to be: tolerable. It would never be the life he had dreamed
of. The perfect, exciting, impossible life he would have had with
her. But it didn't have to be. He carried too many lost lives with
him to live as carefree as he once had. His life had tallied him
into a new person, a man who couldn't go back to before.

William had mused one evening about how perfect he and
Annaleigh had been together. He had never believed in fate, but

Annaleigh had, and she had told him once how she was sure the angels had designed them for one another. But they had grown jealous of their love—a love too large and powerful, a love that exceeded their own plans and expectations—and they'd wanted her back.

One day, hopefully a very long time from now, they would have him back, too.

CHAPTER 27

A Future

SUMMER WARMED THE MOUNTAINS. THE rains had departed, leaving the woods greener than William had ever seen them. The world looked new, the trees and flowers given a fresh start. That's what he wanted—a new beginning to find his stability again, to find his reason.

That's one of the feelings he missed most—the understanding, the sense of purpose. He'd understood life when he'd been with Annaleigh. Even when life had been gritty and awful, he'd felt capable by her side. He knew how to spend his time, where he would invest every ounce of energy and emotion. He had a passion, a drive, just knowing she loved him back. It was an impossible thought that she were to love him, and yet, she did.

The thought gave him wings, made him indestructible.

Without her, he was free-floating. He needed grounding.

On a particularly humid afternoon, William grew restless in the cramped cabin.

"I'm going on a hike," he told Mary, filling a small knapsack with provisions. "I'll be back before it gets dark."

From the stuffed chair in the library, Mary craned her head. "Are you sure?" She locked eyes with Annaleigh, raising her eyebrows in a silent question. *Is this a good idea?*

"I just need to stretch my legs," he said. "If I'm not back in a few hours, you have my permission to send out a search party."

"William..." Mary's tone was warning. She closed her book and went to see everything he was packing.

"I'm kidding, Mary. I'll be back."

"Promise?" She held out her pinky. He hadn't sworn to her like this since they were children, but it brought a smile to him now.

"Promise," he said, locking their pinkies. "Before it gets dark."

The woods were just the escape William needed. As he picked his way through the dark, deep, twisting paths of the mountain, he found himself alone with his thoughts. But he was never truly alone—Annaleigh followed next to him, silent, unseen. She'd become his guardian angel, and though he was never sure she was actually with him, he could swear he felt her presence. It grew particularly strong at night, when the moon was fat and low in the sky. He spoke to her often, held a one-sided conversation where he could only imagine her responses. It helped him to think things through out loud with her.

"I don't know what I'm to do without you," he said to the trees.

Annaleigh nodded, brushed her fingers over his shoulder, down his arm. "Me neither."

"I don't want to waste the time I have. I want to make it count for you. I want to live *for you*. I just don't know how."

"You'll find a way," she answered. The wind lifted, and he could almost make out the sound of her voice.

The farther he hiked away from the cabin, the further he felt from his problems. He climbed up, scaling the faces of rocks as he pulled himself closer to heaven. When he made it to the absolute peak, just miles away from the cabin, he sat.

The sky was perfectly clear. There were no clouds in sight, only circling birds and the occasional butterfly. The sky was so blue and so close. It seemed lower today, as if there were a million angels looking over him and the weight had lowered the ceiling of the universe. He felt small; he felt insignificant.

Looking over the rolling waves of plains below him, he sorted through his thoughts, trying to organize them into some semblance of order. He would live for Annaleigh, have a life of honor that would make her proud. That would make Sara proud—and Mary, too.

He wanted to help people—to stop the pain he felt from happening to anyone else ever again. He wanted to save lives. There was something about that idea that made his heart swell. If he could save even one life, perhaps it would stitch the hole he had in his heart—the part of him that ripped with loss.

William had always been intelligent, but his smarts lay more in wit than subjects of significance. School, then? Yes, that would have to be it.

He watched the town tucked between two farms in the plains under his feet. He saw the comings and goings of tiny people and their tiny lives as he began to plan his.

The Army, perhaps, would be the place to start. He could enlist his services, serve as a paramedic. They could train him, and after he had finished his duty, he could become a doctor. His town only had one really great doctor, and his services were expensive—too expensive for most of his neighbors and friends back home. He could work for a much lower rate. He didn't need the money, didn't want it. He'd seen people sell their houses for treatment, become destitute for a simple bottle of medicine.

He would never turn anyone away. He could help people— *really* help them.

"A doctor," he mused out loud.

"You would be brilliant," Annaleigh said. "Absolutely brilliant."

As the afternoon cooled, he collected himself and his thoughts and returned to Mary. It wasn't even twilight yet when he walked back into the cabin, tossed his knapsack on the table, and made his announcement.

"I want to go home."

Mary dropped the bowl she was washing and it broke at her feet. "Home?" she asked, her eyes widening.

"I think it's time," he said. "I'm done hiding out here. I want to go home. I have things to do."

He explained his plans of enlisting, but Mary couldn't keep her eyes on him. She looked between his smile and Annaleigh's matching one, and the worry that had been hanging over her for months evaporated. He was planning for the future again. He was doing something that would quiet his mind and soothe his soul. He would be a *doctor*.

A vision overtook her there, and she had to close her eyes to the intensity of it.

Mary saw William, a stethoscope around his neck and a syringe in his hands. He stood over a child, a small girl so dark with soot that her eyes were the only clean thing. With careful, practiced hands, he wiped a cloth over the child's arm and plunged in the syringe. The girl didn't cry at all, but the mother did, enveloping William in a great hug with weeps of gratitude. She nearly laughed aloud at the image of William awkwardly hugging the woman back before he moved on to the next patient, one of dozens in a long row of hospital beds.

The scene shifted, and he was packing his equipment back in his doctor bag. As he put away his things, he paused, reached in the bag, and retrieved the locket. It was clasped around the handle of the bag, and Mary saw that it had been engraved with Annaleigh's name.

When Mary opened her eyes again, she was crying.

"Mary, I'll only be gone for a few months, and then I'll be home. I can start a practice in town. It could help a lot of—"

She waved her hands at him, shaking her head. "I know. No, William. It's perfect. It's *perfect*. You'll be great."

"He'll be incredible," Annaleigh added softly.

"You'll be *incredible*," Mary repeated. "Annaleigh would be so proud."

"I am," she said, smiling. "I've never been prouder."

CHAPTER 28

A Return

ALMOST FIVE MONTHS AFTER THEY had left, William returned home with Mary.

Samuel met the siblings at the door, helping William carry in the last of Mary's luggage. They stacked her bags at the bottom of the stairs as Mary went through the house, turning on all of the lights and opening all of the curtains in the front of the house. William stood in front of the open door, looking out over the lawn. He was careful not to look too near the lake though. He wasn't ready for the severity of that memory just yet.

A hand clapped down on his shoulder, and William turned to face Samuel.

"We all miss her," he told William. "She was a light like no other. The world will always be a little darker without her."

William nodded and looked back to the doorway. "This is where I first kissed her."

Samuel stood next to him, smiling. "I remember. You should have seen her face after you left. You'd think you were some dream of hers come to life."

"She was *my* dream," William said. "I had waited so long to kiss her. I didn't think I'd ever work up the nerves to do so. Then she started yelling at me. Remember how she yelled at me?"

Samuel laughed. "She had quite a mouth."

"And I knew—in that moment, I *knew*. She was it." He pictured that day in his mind, remembered the blaze of her furious eyes as she'd scolded him for leaving without so much as a note. She hadn't given him a note when she'd left. "I thought in that moment that I had to kiss her. I was scared she'd hit me, but I didn't care. It would have been worth it."

"I *should* have smacked you." Annaleigh stood in front of him, a sloppy smile on her face. "But it was the best birthday present I had ever gotten."

"She was unlike anyone else I've ever known," Samuel added. "You laughed around her more than I'd ever heard you your entire life. That girl carved a smile out of even your most dour moods." He cleared his throat, fighting off emotion. "We will all miss her more than you know, Master Calloway."

William shook his head, pulled a hand down his face, and turned to face Samuel once more. "Call me William, Samuel. No one ever does anymore."

"Of course, William." Samuel nodded and left to carry the luggage up to Mary's bedroom.

Evening fell fast. The first night back in his room was unbearable. His pillows still smelled like jasmine, like her. He couldn't even consider sleeping in the guest room that Mary had transformed into Annaleigh's bedroom, so William ended up sleeping on the stairs. The next morning, Mary found him leaning on the banister with a blanket wrapped around his shoulders, Sara and Annaleigh watching over him a few steps down.

That night had been the worst of it. He'd nearly slipped back into himself, as he had in the mountains, but he focused on the locket. He'd pull it from his pocket, study it, and remember.

He had a purpose now. He had people to save. He had a future.

It grew easier over time. The pain dulled to something endurable. As long as they kept the drapes closed to the windows that looked over the lake, William was fine. William was *becoming* fine again.

The second week after they'd arrived home, William started leaving the house again. At first, he could only step outside a few feet before he had the urge to go back inside. He felt like there was a rope around his middle, as if he were on a tether that only gave him so much room to roam before he was tugged back. It was a nervousness that he was unfamiliar with, and he only found a modicum of solace back at home.

His lead grew longer though. The few steps stretched into a mile. Then he was able to make it out to town. His trips became longer and longer, and he settled into the anxiety that hummed through him over not having Annaleigh by his side. Only Mary knew he never went to the market alone.

Even after William was able to leave the house without hesitation, he still steered clear of the paths that led to the lake. He closed the curtains in the carriage whenever he had to take a road that passed the water, but he was getting out. Mary took that as a good sign; Annaleigh took it as a miracle. Things were starting to turn around.

William was doing so much better with his trips into the market. People stopped and chatted with him, and only occasionally did they mention Annaleigh. But when they did, his heart would race and he would grow very still, very nervous. His fingers found the locket and traced the pattern over and over again until he could calm down, until the memory of her didn't send him fleeing to the familiar corners of his house.

He tried to be stronger than that. Sometimes he managed to conquer the feelings of dread, of despair that tugged him down. But one afternoon at the market, his strength splintered. The young son of the woman running the fruit stand had been watching him. The redheaded boy saw as William turning the locket over and over in his hand, and he pointed to it curiously, his fingers reaching out to take it.

"Is that *your* necklace?" he asked.

William pulled back, shock across his face. Without an answer, he rushed from the market, to his carriage, and back home. A place where he could hide from people's questions, from their apologies over Annaleigh. Apologies he didn't want to hear. Apologies that never seemed to go away.

Those who didn't mention Annaleigh directly held the thought of her between their pinched brows and downturned mouths. The pitying looks they gave him when he passed were enough to make his skin bead with cool sweat. The stares were enough to push him back inside until he could get control of himself again.

He stayed home, locked in his room for nearly a week before he came out again. He had breakfasts with Mary but still skipped dinner. Then he started coming to dinner—infrequently, but it was another step forward. Most nights, he was even able to keep the food down.

The next week, he tried to make a go at visiting the market again. Annaleigh followed him into town, walking at his heels and smiling as he slowly came back out of himself. When he would see something in the store windows that reminded him of Annaleigh, he would tense up and look back to the carriage. Early on, he would leave at the slightest reminder of her, but he grew stronger, and the signs of her—the remainders of the life she'd left behind—turned from something he dreaded to something he sought out.

He smiled more, he laughed more, and his posture straightened again. He began shaving regularly, eating, drinking, joking around with the children who played in the center of town.

William was returning to himself once again, and Annaleigh was amazed at his strength. He was so much *more* than she'd ever given him credit for.

CHAPTER 29

A Story

ON A SWELTERING SUMMER EVENING just before all of the stalls and stores shut down, William made his final stroll down the busy street in the middle of town, arm in arm with Mary. The flower stand was still open, brimming with bright yellow jasmines, the same flowers Annaleigh had worn at their wedding. The same flowers her bouquet had been made of.

When the fragrance of the flowers lifted on the wind, William was instantly transported back to the last morning he'd spent with Annaleigh—the way she'd smelled in his arms, the light whisper of fabric between their skin.

It was almost too much. His knees felt weak at the sharp reminder of her, and he could have collapsed to the cobbles. He pulled out the locket again, pressed it to his lips. He was no longer desperate for her to return to him—he knew she was gone, that it was better that way—but whispering to the locket had become a habit of his when he thought of her.

Mary put her hand at his back, worried that he would cave under his grief like he had so many times already. But he stood strong, his heart beating in his ears, his blood pounding through his body reminding him how alive he was.

The woman at the flower stand noticed him and smiled. "Would you like a flower?"

He nodded and pulled out folded bills, but she raised her hand and shook her head.

"No need. Take as many as you want," she said. "I'll have to be getting rid of them soon anyway. They're past their date and starting to wilt."

She and her husband helped them load up two baskets of the yellow flowers and take them back to the carriage.

"These are beautiful flowers," Mary said. "I can't wait to arrange them." She turned to Will, grabbed his hand in hers, and squeezed. "Will, they remind me so much of Annaleigh."

"Thank you," William said to anyone who heard.

The woman nodded at the locket he still held in his hand. "What a beautiful locket."

On instinct, he nearly hid it from her, but this time, something stopped him.

Unnoticed next to Mary, Annaleigh watched as he lifted it up and let it spin in the last glint of the setting sun. Surrounded by the warm scent of Annaleigh and so many reminders, William found a story of his own falling from his lips. The story of how his mother had come to the locket, how it had been Annaleigh's once he'd proposed.

"She was a beautiful girl," the woman said. "She was loved by everyone."

William smiled. "She was, wasn't she?"

He helped Mary into the carriage and they were on their way home. As they were passing the lake, Mary went to close the curtains, but William held out his hand, pushing the fabric back. The lake spread out next to them, wide and serene. The hair on the back of his neck stood up, the fingers of a ghost trailing up his spine, but he didn't feel sick. He didn't have the urge to yell, to run and run until he was so far away from the water that he could pretend it didn't exist.

A peacefulness swam through his veins. He rapped on the roof of the carriage and they came to a stop.

"There's something I have to do," he said to Mary.

She looked between him, the flowers, and Annaleigh who sat so closely next to him that she was shocked he couldn't feel her there. She was worried about him being alone after the market—after the flowers, the memories of Annaleigh that she knew lived just under the surface of his skin—but his gray eyes were not stormy with misery. They were clear and bright, shining with optimism.

Mary nodded once. "All right."

He climbed out of the carriage, taking one of the baskets of flowers with him before closing the door and sending Mary on her way. He watched as the carriage wove back home, bouncing on the uneven road. He waited for the dust to settle before he moved.

William, with a specter at his shoulder, spun around to face the memories that had haunted him through so many sleepless nights: the lake.

Part 6

For the moon never beams, without bringing me dreams
Of the beautiful Annabel Lee;
And the stars never rise, but I feel the bright eyes
Of the beautiful Annabel Lee;
And so, all the night-tide, I lie down by the side
Of my darling — my darling — my life and my bride,
In her sepulchre there by the sea —
In her tomb by the sounding sea.

— Stanza VI, *Annabel Lee* by Edgar Allan Poe

CHAPTER 30

The Goodbye

PAST BATTLED PRESENT IN WILLIAM'S mind. Though it was a hot summer day and the twilight sky was still a bright pink, he saw the cold, dark night of his wedding.

Hefting the basket of flowers up to his hip, he walked, numb, out on the dock of the lake. He looked over the water, so peaceful and undisturbed. He remembered the summers they'd spent swimming there, the times they'd taken the small boat her father owned out on the water, how they would tease Mary, rocking it side to side until they nearly tipped over.

And of course, he remembered the night he'd lost her. It hurt less than he'd thought it would.

He dumped the basket of flowers out, the petals and stems dropping to the water and floating away.

"For you, Annaleigh," he said, watching the jasmine spread wider and wider, dotting the deep-blue water with brilliant yellow. It looked like the sky, dusted with spectacular stars. A universe at his feet.

Without really thinking about it, he slid out of his shoes, rolled up the sleeves of his shirt, and dove in, just as he had that loathsome night. This time, though, he didn't try to dive to the bottom. He let himself float, let the lake rock him gently across its surface as he gripped the locket in his fist. The water was warm, and he closed his eyes, drifting off with the flowers.

Floating on his back, he let the happy memories of the lake thaw the frozen dread he kept locked inside of him. He warmed from the inside out, the past becoming a softer memory. There were no more sharp edges he had to avoid, nothing he had to pretend to forget, to ignore. He remembered it all, happy and sad. The times he'd gone swimming with Annaleigh and how she could beat him in any swimming competition—who could swim the fastest, who could hold their breath the longest...

He couldn't believe he had lost her here. A small part of him would always blame himself for being too late to save her. As he floated on, carried on the surface of the water with the flowers, he had one last conversation with the memory of her.

"I will never forgive myself," he said. "Not entirely."

"There's nothing to forgive," Annaleigh answered.

Finally, after all this time, he heard her voice. But he told himself that she wasn't there. She couldn't be. Surely his mind was playing tricks on him—wishful thinking that she had finally returned to him. He hadn't seen her since the cabin though, and he hoped she was somewhere better. She deserved to be somewhere better.

"Nothing was your fault, William," she said, and his heart thrilled at the sound of his name on her lips again, even just in memory. "My life had run its course. There was nothing you could've done to save me," she continued. "Fate doesn't have to be fair or make sense. It just has to happen, one way or another."

"I wish I could have rewritten the fates. I would have rearranged the stars for you," he said.

Annaleigh watched him from the edge of the dock, silent tears falling down her face. She saw the shift as he came to terms with all that he had lost. That last afternoon on the mountain had changed him. Feeling so small, feeling insignificant but still strong... It had been good for him. He was finally beginning to see the beauty in himself that she always had. Perhaps losing her, having to come to terms with a pain so boundless, had done something amazing in him, too. It had turned his world upside down, and he'd started noticing things he never had before.

He saw how wealth did nothing for him but offer security. He saw those around him who had so little live a life that was no less than his. He read the news of children starving and soldiers over in England coming home wounded and alone.

That afternoon, when he had told Mary his plans to join the Army as a doctor, she'd heard the power return to his voice, the conviction. He would serve as a paramedic. He would make sure no one else had to say goodbye to loved ones before their time. William wanted to be greater than himself, to leave an impact beyond his own life. Annaleigh knew he was more than capable.

The pain that had ripped him in two had elicited a desire to heal, and he would be leaving in the fall, right around the time of her birthday. Fate was funny that way.

"This is who you were always meant to be," Annaleigh said, looking over at him and imagining him as a paramedic, bandaging the wounded with his words and his skillful hands.

Mary had described her vision to her briefly one night, and she wished more than anything that she could stay to see it. But her time was running out; he didn't need her anymore.

Surrounded by flowers, peacefully floating under the setting summer sun, he looked like hope incarnate. He would do so much good in this world.

When the sun hid itself for the night and the lake became too chilly to be comfortable, William swam out of the water. He walked up the shore barefoot. The locket swung from his grip, keeping tempo with his heart.

He ducked into the woods and found the tree where he had proposed to Annaleigh. It had grown larger since he'd been gone, and its branches were no longer spindly and bare, but weighed down with wide, green leaves and fragrant flowers. He touched the trunk of the tree, closing his eyes and remembering the kiss they'd shared here, hidden from the world.

He was done hiding now. He wanted to be seen and make his life count—no matter how much time he had left. Five days, five years, five decades... It didn't matter to him. Every day would contain a lifetime worth of living. He wouldn't regret a single second, because this life had to be enough.

At his feet, he found a small, sharp rock. He placed the locket back around his neck and picked up the rock, bringing it to the rough bark of the trunk. In his sloppy handwriting, with his shaking hand, he carved her name just under the lowest branch. When he finished, he ran his thumb over the letters, brushing away the curled pieces of shaved wood.

"Goodbye, Annaleigh," he said, stepping back. He spoke to the tree, picturing just how she had fit to it before. Annaleigh stood in front of him, watching his eyes and noticing the newfound strength in them.

"We loved with a love that was more than love—" He lowered his eyes to his feet, looked out over the lake. "You will be in my heart. Always."

"Our souls will not ever dissever," Annaleigh answered him. She focused all of her love, all of the strength she had left, and leaned forward to place one final kiss right at the corner of his lips. It warmed her and it sent his heart soaring.

When she stepped back, he raised his face, searching for the source of the touch. But he didn't have to be a seer like Mary to know that it was his Annaleigh. She had given him her blessing to go on living, and he promised her he would do just that. He would not take a moment of his life for granted.

He would live enough for both of them.

As he made his way up the grassy hill, away from the woods and his past, Sara joined Annaleigh, emerging from the darkness behind her. Together, they walked back to the edge of the lake.

"The impact you left on his life is immeasurable," Sara said, looking after her son.

Annaleigh smiled, tears in his eyes. "The impact he left on *my* life is immeasurable."

"Thank you for saving my son."

Annaleigh looked at Sara, shared one last hug, and said her goodbyes. She could feel the last of her substantiality slipping away, but it didn't scare her anymore. She welcomed whatever would greet her after this world—whether it was nothing or everything. A peacefulness washed over her like a breeze welcoming her to join them in the clouds.

"Rest, sweet child," Sara said. "Be at peace."

With an exhale, Annaleigh disappeared on the wind. She caressed Mary's spirit as she left, passed a soft hand over the cheek of her father, the arm of her mother, and she was gone.

Annaleigh's soul lit up the moon, and with burning fingers, she rearranged the stars for William.

Acknowledgments

I owe a few thank you's to some really spectacular people —

To Kellie. Without you, this book wouldn't exist. Also, several headaches wouldn't exist, but I consider it a fair trade. Thank you for convincing me to be a little mad.

To Mickey, my editor, my savior. I really lucked out when I found you!

To my teachers along the way who introduced my infatuation with poetry and Edgar Allan Poe. Thank you.

To my family. Thank you for your patience and (over)confidence in my writing. In particular, I offer my thanks and apologies to my sister, Jessica. Thank you for tolerating the number of times I read *Tell Tale Heart* to you while you were still in elementary school. I don't know why I thought a story about a beating heart beneath a floorboard was an appropriate bedtime story for a child, but you never stopped me.

Thank you to the WordNerds, for their support and encouragement. Meghan Jashinsky, thank you for reading the early (really rough) version of *Madly, Deeply*.

And finally to you, the reader, for simply believing.

Thank you.

About the Author

Erica Crouch is a young adult and new adult author from the colorful city of Baltimore, Maryland. Currently, she is studying English and Creative Writing with a specialization in Fiction at Southern New Hampshire University. She is the cofounder and head of editorial services/design at Patchwork Press. http://erica.patchwork-press.com

---

MORE TITLES BY ERICA CROUCH
Ignite (Ignite #1)
Entice (Ignite #1.5)

MORE TITLES FROM PWP
The Hitchhiker Series, by Kellie Sheridan
Beautiful Madness Series, by Kellie Sheridan
Grimm Tales Series, by Janna Jennings
Orenda, by Ruth Silver
Dead Girl Walking, by Ruth Silver
The Rising, by Terra Harmony
Solving for Ex, by Leigh Ann Kopans